汉 英 双 语

我可否把你比作夏日绮丽

莎士比亚十四行诗全集

Shakespeare's Sonnets

［英］威廉·莎士比亚＼著

夏 晗＼译

九州出版社

JIUZHOUPRESS

图书在版编目（CIP）数据

我可否把你比作夏日绮丽 ：莎士比亚十四行诗全集：汉文、英文 /（英）威廉·莎士比亚著；夏晗译 . -- 北京 ：九州出版社，2022.11
ISBN 978-7-5225-1449-9

Ⅰ．①我… Ⅱ．①威… ②夏… Ⅲ．①十四行诗－诗集－英国－中世纪－汉、英 Ⅳ．① I561.23

中国版本图书馆 CIP 数据核字（2022）第 221537 号

我可否把你比作夏日绮丽：莎士比亚十四行诗全集（汉英双语）

作　　者	［英］威廉·莎士比亚 著
译　　者	夏　晗
责任编辑	周红斌
出版发行	九州出版社
地　　址	北京市西城区阜外大街甲 35 号（100037）
发行电话	（010）68992190/3/5/6
网　　址	www.jiuzhoupress.com
电子信箱	jiuzhou@jiuzhoupress.com
印　　刷	廊坊市祥丰印刷有限公司
开　　本	710 毫米 × 1000 毫米　16 开
印　　张	21
字　　数	450 千字
版　　次	2022 年 11 月第 1 版
印　　次	2022 年 12 月第 1 次印刷
书　　号	ISBN 978-7-5225-1449-9
定　　价	58.00 元

译　序

在浩瀚的世界诗歌海洋，有一颗明珠熠熠闪烁，与我国李白、杜甫为代表的诗歌河汉巨星相映成辉，这就是欧洲文艺复兴时期英国著名剧作家、诗人莎士比亚的十四行诗。作为文艺复兴时期的代表人物，莎士比亚与其同时代的中国剧作家汤显祖一样，以其卷帙浩繁的剧作饮誉世界，但其诗歌，尤其是他的十四行诗，同样大放异彩，展现出无穷的魅力，吸引着人们阅读鉴赏、研究翻译。笔者也成为了其中一员，在阅读鉴赏莎翁十四行诗的同时，将其陆续译中文。现将其呈献给广大读者，希望本译为读者阅读莎士比亚十四行诗带来新体验和新感悟。

十四行诗与莎士比亚十四行诗

十四行诗（Sonnet）又译商籁体，源于意大利的一种格律严谨的抒情诗体，由文艺复兴先驱、"人文主义之父"彼特拉克在其诗歌创作中使其臻于完善，因此又称彼特拉克体，之后传到欧洲各国，被纷纷效仿。

彼特拉克的十四行诗形式整齐，音韵优美，结构上分为两部分。第一部分由两段四行诗（quatrain）组成，韵式为 abbaabba；第二部分由两段三行诗组成，韵式为 cdccdc 或 cdcdcd 等（实际上是自由用韵的六行诗），一般为抑扬格；其内容以歌颂爱情、表现人文主义思想为主要特征。

十四行诗传入英国后，以莎士比亚为代表的英国诗人在诗歌创作中对彼特拉克体进行改造，逐步形成了新的十四行诗制式：第一部分由三个四行诗组成，押间韵，第二部分由两句组成，押联韵，全部为五音步抑扬格，其结构精妙，音乐性强，起承转合自如，最后两句对全诗内容主题进行概括总结（当然也有少数例外，如莎士比亚十四行诗第十三首、第三十二首、第三十五首、第三十九首、第四十六首、第六十五首、第七十一首、第九十七首、第一二一首、第一三三首等），这便是莎士比亚十四行诗特定制式。

莎士比亚十四行诗共有一五四首。但应说明一点，从严格意义上讲，其中有三首并非典型的莎体十四行诗：第九十九首为十五行，多出第一行导语；第一二六首不仅行数只有十二行，而且韵律制式也与十四行诗不同，实际为一首英雄体；第一四五首，虽然是十四行，但每行只有四音步，也不是典型的莎体十四行诗的制式。

在内容上，一般认为，第一至第一二六首，通过写一位贵族美少，赞美他的美貌，以歌颂爱情的笔触抒发诗人与其真诚友情；第一二七至第一五二首通过写诗人对一位黑发褐肤女郎的一往情深抒发其真挚的爱情。至于第一五三和第一五四两首，是单独的主题，笔者认为是两首寓言式爱情诗。

莎士比亚十四行诗内涵深邃，意境幽微，彰显人文主义情怀，歌颂真善美主题，倾情讴歌生命、爱情、友情和真情，把爱情和友情作为美的源泉和载体尽情赞颂，殷殷关切生命和生命的赓续，让真善美因生命的赓续而成为永恒，堪称对真善美的一首首赞歌！

关于本译

作为莎士比亚十四行诗的一个新译版本，旨在力求通过用畅美的语言诠释其深邃内涵，实现达意传神，再现其优美意境；努力实现准确翻译，贴切表达。准确翻译是翻译的第一定律，也是做到达意传神的基础。如果译不达意，翻译也就失去了自身的意义和价值。要做到准确翻译，首先要准确理解原文。这对于莎士比亚十四诗的翻译来说并非易事。大家知道，莎士比亚十四行诗除了错综纷繁的语言结构（普遍的多重复合、倒装、省略等）和复杂多变的意象外，还包括中古英语句法和词汇，给读者理解造成一定障碍。例如，仅就词汇而言，诗中有些词虽然与现代英语拼写同形，但却是古义，若按照现代英语的理解去翻译，自然译不达意，读了会感到牵强，甚至语焉不详，不知所云。譬如莎士比亚十四行诗第三十九首有这样一句话（分排在六行——结构不可谓不复杂）：

> O absence, what a torment wouldst thou prove,
> Were it not thy sour leisure gave sweet leave
> To entertain the time with thoughts of love,
> Which time and thoughts so sweetly doth deceive,
> And that thou teachest how to make one twain
> By praising him here who doth hence remain!

其中第一行的 prove 一词系古义（have sb.）experience/suffer，而非"证明"；而第四行的 deceive 也系古义，意为 beguile away［消磨，度过（时光）；使（时光等）轻松愉快地度过］，而非"欺骗"。如果按照后者的意思翻译，自然会词不达意。因此，上面的第一行的准确翻译应该是：

> O absence, what a torment wouldst thou prove,
> 噢，别离啊！你将会使我忍受何等的痛苦！

整个句子（六行）可翻译如下：

> 噢，别离啊！要不是你用枯燥的闲暇让我得以甜蜜独处，
> 使我沉浸在充满爱的情思的时光里
> 甜美地怡享时光和情思惝惝流逝；
> 要不是你教会我如何化形单为影双，
> 　　使我可以在此对远别的吾爱倾情赞扬[①]，
> 　　不然，那将会使我忍受何等的愁伤！

至于意境再现，则需要注重诗性语言再造，凸显诗歌语言的艺术张力。例如，诗歌语言的艺术特征之一就是含蓄婉转。为凸显这一特征，就不能按字面意思直白翻译，必须婉转抒发、含蓄表达，"发掘出"其在原诗语境下所表达的深层意蕴，才能使译文富有诗性和意境。

例如，莎士比亚十四行诗第七十一首中有这样一句话（分排版在六行）：

O, if, I say, you look upon this verse
When I perhaps compounded am with clay,
Do not so much as my poor name rehearse.
But let your love even with my life decay,
Lest the wise world should look into your moan
And mock you with me after I am gone.

[①] 如本诗开头所述，他与其爱共为一体时，顾忌"赞美你时又岂不是也在赞美自己"，现在一经分开，便可无所顾忌地对其爱倾情赞扬。——译者注

其中的第四行，我曾读到过这样的译文：

愿你的爱与我的生命一同腐烂。

译文把 decay 按字面意义译成"腐烂"，应当说没有选错义项，但从译诗的角度看，说"爱和生命腐烂"，总觉得少了几分意境或诗意。

笔者将其译为：

姑且让你的爱与我的生命一同化作青烟飞逝。

这里，把 decay 译为"化作青烟飞逝"，"发掘出" decay 在原诗的深层意蕴，克服了直白翻译的弊病，赋予语言以含蓄婉转特征。

至于本书全部译文是否达到了达意传神和意境再现两个既定目标，自然由读者、学者来评判。当然，翻译中如有任何不妥，也请读者批评指正。

此外，关于本译，还有必要向读者做以下几点说明。

第一，译文采用新诗形式。众所周知，莎士比亚十四行诗为格律英诗，本译采用新诗来翻译，这也是迄今为止格律英诗汉译的通行做法。一方面，笔者认为这样更能让译语传达原诗的诗魂和意境；另一方面，由于汉语格律诗字数（五言或七言等）以及严苛的格律（包括平仄、粘对、押韵等）限制，把英语律诗译成汉语格律诗几乎是不可能的，而且也没有必要。即使牵强地译成了汉语格律诗，也未必能很好地传达原诗的内涵和意境。当然，将少数几首英语律诗译成汉语律诗做一些尝试未尝不可，但难以推而广之，尽管笔者坚持汉语律诗英译时要译成英语格律诗。笔者在诗歌翻译实践中发现，英语格律诗不太适合翻译成中国的格律诗，而中国的格律诗很适合翻译成英语格律诗。

既然是采用新诗形式，译文就不刻意追求行长等度。前面已经提到，莎士比亚十四行诗的格律制式为五音步抑扬格，每行的音步数是等度的，但我们的译文并不刻意追求行长（每行字数）相同，尽管笔者的译文中不少系行长等度。这样，有的整齐划一，有的则错落有致，看上去似乎全书风格不统一，实则不然，这是因为译文诗行分行以原诗句子或语节为基础，不去刻意通过对自然顺畅的语句增减字词而勉强凑齐；当然，其自然整齐的，我们也不去刻意做成错落有致的形式；而是始终把重心放在译文的意义准确和意境再现，努力实现原作诗意的完美传达。

第二，力求押韵，但不苛求。不论是格律诗还是新诗，押韵会增加诗的音乐性，提升诗的审美效果。我国的格律诗特别是近体诗和国外的格律诗，押韵是其基本要素和基本特征，并且均有严格的押韵格式或制式。新诗的诞生，打破了格律诗的押韵制式和韵律传统。一是行长无需等度，二是有韵无制，开辟了诗歌新境界。本译既然是采用新诗形式，那么押韵也就不是固定制式，译文力求押韵，但不过分苛求，以免因韵害意，但在总体上做到押韵。

说到译诗押韵，有的译者强调追求原诗的押韵格式，甚至有人追求与原诗韵声相似，这显然有些胶柱鼓瑟。因为诗的韵律是通过和谐的声音来营造语言的音乐美，并且便于吟诵、记忆。两种语言，特别是不同语系的两种语言，表达同一个意思的字词发音存在云泥之别，套用原韵或原韵制式几近不可能，而且也无此必要。正确的做法是，按照译语表达需要，再造一种新的韵律格式，使诗歌的音乐性得以完美呈现——呈现的是诗韵美，而不是呈现原诗的韵律格式。例如，笔者采用连韵（句句押韵）制式①翻译莎士比亚十四行诗第十八首如下：

---

① 包括邻韵和近韵。

018

我可否把你比作夏日绮丽？

其实你比夏日更温柔娇昳。

狂风恣肆摧残五月的花蕾，

夏日时光短暂会匆匆离去；

苍天眸子常使人灼热难御，

它金色的面庞亦常被阴翳。

夏日的群芳百媚也会衰替，

或因偶然或因时变而枯毙。

唯你绵亘的夏日永不逝去，

你天生的质丽也永不凋靡。

死神也难让你行游其辖域，

你将伴随这诗章千古不息。

　　只要人类双目不瞑，呼吸不止，

　　这诗将长存，亦使你流芳百世！

　　不难看出，译文并未在用原诗的押韵格式 abab, cdcd, efef, gg。虽然译文与原文的押韵制式不同，但诗的韵律充分彰显诗歌的音乐特性。可见，译诗押韵未必套用原文的韵律制式，也能够使原诗的音乐性得以展现。

　　对此，我们还可以用汉译英的例子加以印证。下面是笔者对李之仪《卜算子》的英译。

卜算子

[宋]李之仪

我住长江头，

君住长江尾。

日日思君不见君，

共饮长江水。

此水几时休，

此恨何时已。

只愿君心似我心，

定不负相思意。

Busuanzi·**Ever-missing**

by Li Zhiyi [Song Dynasty]

I live in the River① reaches upper,

And thou abid'st in its reaches lower,

I miss thee e'ery day e'en thou out of my sight

Though we drink the water of the same river.

When will run out the River's flow?

And when will end my grave woe?

I wish thou truly lovest me as I love thee,

Not deceive my deep love shouldst thou.

---

① The River, referring the Yangtze River.

译文在中国诗歌学会公众号上推出后，有读者给予高度赞誉，称"把中国经典诗词翻译得如此传神到位，不是一般的功夫"。读者的这种称赞除了对译文忠实传达原诗内涵和意境外，也应包括其音韵表征的音乐特征。译文虽未沿用原诗（词）的 abcb 押韵格式，而是根据翻译实际采用 aaba 的韵式，同样使原诗的音乐之美得以充分彰显。

第三，依据权威版本翻译。本译本依据 Random House 1975 年出版的 *The Complete Works of William Shakespeare* 中收录的 Sonnets 文本翻译，力求做到准确无误。

另外，要特别说明一点，由于十四行诗原诗并没有标题，只是对每首诗标以序号，很不便记忆。本译在编排上，除仍对每首诗标以序号外，将其首行兼作标题用黑体编排，以便于读者记忆。

莎士比亚十四行诗是英语文学乃至世界文学的瑰宝，如同我国唐代以李白、杜甫为代表的诗人把中国诗歌推向了中国文学的巅峰，莎士比亚以其十四行诗把英语诗歌推向英语文学的高峰，是英语诗歌史上的里程碑，以其内涵深邃、感情丰沛、语言优美享誉世界，自四百多年前问世以来，经久不衰，历久弥新，依然以其无穷魅力吸引着广大读者阅读、思考。笔者本着"信达雅""译文信息等价性与传递性"①等翻译原则，力求向读者奉上一个畅美传神的中译本，使莎士比亚十四行诗这个百世经典在更广阔的审美空间实现与读者心灵的沟通，使读者领略莎士比亚十四行诗的真谛与魅力，激发对人生、对爱情、对友情更真切的感悟与深刻的思考。

译 者

2022 年 10 月 16 日

---

① 冯志杰，冯玫萍：译文的信息等价性与传递性：翻译的二元基本标准 [J]. 中国翻译，1996（2）:18-21

目　录

CONTENTS

To the Only Begetter of These Ensuing Sonnets

Mr. W. H.

All Happiness and That Eternity Promised by Our Ever-lasting Poet
Wisheth the Well-wishing Adventurer in Setting Forth

T. T.

献给本商籁体诗集出版的唯一促成者

W. H. 先生

愿他福星永照，克享我们的不朽诗人所冀之永世盛名！

心怀良愿而毅然付梓的

T. T. 恭祝

威廉·莎士比亚

William Shakespeare

(1564.4.23—1616.4.23）

001

From fairest creatures we desire increase,

That thereby beauty's rose might never die,

But as the riper should by time decrease,

His tender heir might bear his memory;

But thou, contracted to thine own bright eyes,

Feed'st thy light's flame with self-substantial fuel,

Making a famine where abundance lies,

Thyself thy foe, to thy sweet self too cruel.

Thou that are now the world's fresh ornament

And only herald to the gaudy spring,

Within thine own bud buriest thy content,

And, tender churl, mak'st waste in niggarding.

     Pity the world, or else this glutton be,

     To eat the world's due, by the grave and thee.

001

愿世间的美丽生灵生生不息，

故而娇媚的玫瑰将永不凋靡。

纵然生命成熟会随天时衰微，

却有风华子嗣将其美质承袭。

你却与自己的眼睛订立婚契[①]，

以己为薪双眸烧出光焰熠熠；

在丰饶之地偏偏制造出荒饥，

对美丽的自己残酷如同对敌。

你是艳美春天的唯一信使，

把当今世界装点得多彩绚丽，

却将美质[②]深藏于自己的蓓蕾，

你这年轻的老吝啬因吝啬而浪费[③]。

　　怜惜这个世界吧，不然你就会像个贪吃鬼，

　　与坟墓一起将子嗣及万物吞噬得一无所遗！

---

① 喻指自恋自爱，不结婚繁衍后代。——译者注

② 美质：这里用以代指具有美质特征的潜在子嗣。——译者注

③ "年轻的老吝啬因吝啬而浪费"：在莎士比亚眼里，如果一个人的美质不通过结婚生子
传给后代，无疑是一种浪费（这一理念在后面的若干首十四行诗中都有体现）；而将其
潜在的美丽子孙"藏于自己的蓓蕾"不加利用（不通过生子把美质传给后代），又无异
于是一种吝啬的行为，所以是"因吝啬而浪费"。"蓓蕾"的英文为 bud，系双关语。"年
轻的老吝啬（鬼）""因吝啬而浪费（或"吝啬地浪费"）均系矛盾修辞法（Oxymoron）。——
译者注

002

When forty winters shall besiege thy brow

And dig deep trenches in thy beauty's field,

Thy youth's proud livery, so gazed on now,

Will be a totter'd weed of small worth held.

Then being asked where all thy beauty lies,

Where all the treasure of thy lusty days,

To say within thine own deep-sunken eyes

Were an all-eating shame and thriftless praise.

How much more praise deserved thy beauty's use

If thou couldst answer, "This fair child of mine

Shall sum my count and make my old excuse,"

Proving his beauty by succession thine.

  This were to be new made when thou art old

  And see thy blood warm when thou feel'st it cold.

002

当四十个严冬围袭你的前额，

在你那美丽的原野深掘沟壑。

你青春骄人的外衣今人歆羡，

明朝将会变成衰草不名一文；

人们会问你当年的美丽何在，

你宝贵的金色年华如今在哪里？

你若说在自己深陷的眼窝里——

无异于彰示你贪吃的羞耻①和对挥霍的炫耀②。

而你若回答："我这美丽的孩子

将赓续我的韶华，解我的老迈心忧"，

证明你的美质已得到薪尽火传，

你因自己的美质得到活用而值得称赞！

　　　如此，在你终老时美质便获重生，

　　　你已然变冷的热血也将再次沸腾。

---

① 贪吃的羞耻：可参考莎士比亚十四行诗第一首的结尾句。——译者注

② 挥霍：可与莎士比亚十四行诗第一首的第十二行互鉴。

003

Look in thy glass, and tell the face thou view'st,

Now is the time that face should form another,

Whose fresh repair if now thou not renew'st,

Thou dost beguile the world, unbless some mother.

For where is she so fair whose unear'd womb

Disdains the tillage of thy husbandry?

Or who is he so fond will be the tomb

Of his self-love, to stop posterity?

Thou art thy mother's glass, and she in thee

Calls back the lovely April of her prime;

So thou through windows of thine age shalt see,

Despite of wrinkles, this thy golden time.

    But if thou live remember'd not to be,

    Die single, and thine image dies with thee.

003

照照镜子看你的面孔是何等模样，

现在已是时候该造一副新的面庞——

再生一副清新稚嫩的美丽容颜，

不然你就是在消靡这世界①，让良女为母无缘②；

如此美丽尤物的未开垦处女地，

怎会拒绝你的精心耕耘？

又有哪位男子汉如此自爱自恋，

愚蠢到把自己变成断子绝孙的荒坟？

你是你母亲的镜子，从你身上

她唤回了自己曾经四月天般的芳华。

同样，你到年迈时虽皱纹满面，但透过暮年的窗扉③，

也可洞见你曾经的锦瑟流年。

　　　如果你不愿让人记住你的一生一世④，

　　　那就只身死吧，连同你的貌美质丽。

---

① 诗人认为，不娶妻生子而独身就是在消靡或毁灭这个世界。诗人的这一理念还见于其
　 十四行诗第十一首。——译者注
② 指不与女性发生关系，即不娶妻生子。倡导娶妻生子，让生命赓续，是莎士比亚十四行
　 诗中的一个重要主题，这体现于他的多首十四行诗。——译者注
③ 暮年的窗扉：喻指年老昏花的眼睛。——译者注
④ 因为他自爱自恋，不结婚生子，自然就无人记住他在世时的过往。——译者注

004

Unthrifty loveliness, why dost thou spend
Upon thyself they beauty's legacy?
Nature's bequest gives nothing but doth lend,
And, being frank, she lends to those are free.
Then, beauteous niggard, why dost thou abuse
The bounteous largess given thee to give?
Profitless usurer, why dost thou use
So great a sum of sums, yet canst not live?
For having traffic with thyself alone,
Thou of thyself thy sweet self dost deceive.
Then how, when Nature calls thee to be gone,
What acceptable audit canst thou leave?
     Thy unused beauty must be tomb'd with thee,
     Which, used, lives th' executor to be.

004

你这挥霍成性可爱可疼的人，

为何把美的遗产全用于自身？

造物主只出借，而不做馈赠，

她虽慷慨却只借与慷慨之人。

你这贪美的吝啬鬼，为何竟把造物主

托付你须转交的美质滥用无遗？

你这不图利①的高利贷放贷人，

为何花尽巨资却仍无法生存？②

因为你只与自己单独做生意③，

欺骗也只是骗了可爱的自己。

当造物主把你召回时，

你怎能把满意的账簿④留给后世？

　　　　你未贷出的美质资本将随你而去，

　　　　而已贷出的美质资本⑤则把美传袭。

---

① 资本不贷出去，自然就不生利；"无法生存"，指自己的生命无法让后代延续。——译者注

② 诗人将美比作"资本"；无法生存，喻指生命无法让后代延续。——译者注

③ 这里喻指不与异性发生关系而自慰。——译者注

④ 在西方以基督教为基础的宗教文化中，认为人在世时必须行善事，否则就欠下上帝的账目，在死时（上帝召回时）入不了天堂。——译者注

⑤ 贷出的美质资本：即遗传给子孙的美。——译者注

005

Those hours, that with gentle work did frame

The lovely gaze where every eye doth dwell,

Will play the tyrants to the very same

And that unfair which fairly doth excel;

For never-resting time leads summer on

To hideous winter and confounds him there;

Sap checked with frost and lusty leaves quite gone,

Beauty o'ersnowed and bareness everywhere:

Then, were not summer's distillation left,

A liquid prisoner pent in walls of glass,

Beauty's effect with beauty were bereft,

Nor it nor no remembrance what it was.

> But flowers distilled, though they with winter meet,
>
> Leese but there show; their substance still lives sweet.

005

时光如同一丝不苟的精工巧匠，
总是雕出万人瞩目的娇颜无双。
但总有一天也会对其横施暴虐，
让其美丽的容颜变得丑陋不堪。
永不停歇的时间老人总把夏日
带到可恶的冬天将其狠狠蹂躏，
引寒霜致草木枯萎、绿叶凋零，
让冬雪覆盖美景，到处一派荒凉。
那时，如果夏日香髓未能提炼
并"囚禁"于玻璃高墙里面①，
美的风韵将随美一道灰飞烟灭，
无以赓续，不给人留下一丝怀念。

　　　香花一经提炼，即使遇到隆冬严寒，
　　　虽没了华丽外表，芬芳亦永驻人间！

---

① 玻璃高墙里面：即瓶子里面，喻指子宫。——译者注

006

Then let not winter's ragged hand deface

In thee thy summer, ere thou be distilled:

Make sweet some vial; treasure thou some place

With beauty's treasure ere it be self-killed.

That use is not forbidden usury,

Which happies those that pay the willing loan;

That's for thyself to breed another thee,

Or ten times happier, be it ten for one;

Ten times thyself were happier than thou art,

If ten of thine ten times refigured thee:

Then what could Death do if thou shouldst depart,

Leaving thee living in posterity?

    Be not self-willed, for thou art much too fair

    To be Death's conquest and make worms thine heir.

006

在你自身的精华未经提炼之前

切勿让严冬的魔爪摧毁你的夏天①。

备好储香瓶②，不待你的精华消失，

将其连同你的美质于某处珍藏。

这并非禁止以牟利为目的的借代，

而是让付息的借贷人获得幸福；

对你而言就是再生出一个自己，

若一能生十，幸福也将徒增十倍。

如果你有十个胜似自己的子嗣，

你的幸福将十倍于现在的自己。

那时，可恶的死神又奈你若何？

即使你死了，也在子孙后代得到赓续。

　　切勿顽固不化，你如此美貌绝伦，

　　莫被死神征服③，让蛆虫当了子孙。

---

① 莎士比亚经常用"夏天"喻指美貌青年或美好年华。可参见其十四行诗第十八首等。——译者注

② 储香瓶：喻指子宫。——译者注

③ 这里诗人所说被死神征服不只是指死亡，更指没有子嗣遗传其美质。——译者注

007

Lo, in the orient when the gracious light

Lifts up his burning head, each under eye

Doth homage to his new-appearing sight,

Serving with looks his sacred majesty;

And having climb'd the steep-up hea'enly hill,

Resembling strong youth in his middle age,

Yet mortal looks adore his beauty still,

Attending on his golden pilgrimage;

But when from highmost pitch, with weary car,

Like feeble age he reeleth from the day,

The eyes,'fore duteous, now converted are

From his low tract and look another way:

>   So thou, thyself, outgoing in thy noon,

>   Unlook'd on diest unless thou get a son.

007

看！日神那火红的头在东方昂起，
在他缓缓升起刚一露出真容之际，
顷刻世间每一双眼睛都向他致敬，
皆以敬仰的神情膜拜这君王至圣。
当他攀上崎岖而高耸入云的山顶，
虽已步入中年，却宛若年少芳龄。
世人对其美貌仍投以倾慕的眼神，
紧紧追随他金光闪闪的天路历程；
但当他乘着疲惫的车驾①越过山巅，
像耄耋老人从白昼蹒跚步入夜晚，
走向落寞，从前对他仰慕的目光
便统统从其身上移开而另觅"新欢"。
　　而你也会是一样，只要一过盛时年华，
　　除非你有子嗣，否则将孤身死于病榻。

---

① 古人认为日神是乘车旅行的。——译者注

008

Music to hear, why hear'st thou music sadly?

Sweets with sweets war not, joy delights in joy,

Why lov'st thou that which thou receiv'st not gladly,

Or else receiv'st with pleasure thine annoy?

If the true concord of well-tunèd sounds,

By unions married, do offend thine ear,

They do but sweetly chide thee, who confounds

In singleness the parts that thou shouldst bear.

Mark how one string, sweet husband to another,

Strikes each in each by mutual ordering;

Resembling sire and child and happy mother,

Who, all in one, one pleasing note do sing:

  Whose speechless song, being many, seeming one,

  Sings this to thee, "Thou single wilt prove none."

008

悦耳的音乐为什么你听了却会悲伤？

甜美与甜美相辅，快乐与快乐相成。

既然不乐意接受，为何又如此钟情，

为何欣然接受所遇的烦恼？

如果有几种美妙的声调和谐不悖，

合奏出美妙的曲调而冒犯了你的耳朵，

那也只不过是温情地责备你

用孤弦毁掉了本该用和弦演奏的乐章。

看！一根弦如丈夫与另外一根弦

如何相互和谐有序弹出美妙的乐曲，

像父亲、儿子和快乐的母亲一起

放声高唱一支悦耳动听的欢歌。

　　这无词的歌异曲同声，都向你高唱：

　　"你若孤身无嗣，那将一切皆空！"

009

Is it for fear to wet a widow's eye

That thou consum'st thyself in single life?

Ah! if thou issueless shalt hap to die,

The world will wail thee like a makeless wife;

The world will be thy widow and still weep

That thou no form of thee hast left behind,

When every private widow well may keep,

By children's eyes, her husband's shape in mind.

Look, what an unthrift in the world doth spend

Shifts but his place, for still the world enjoys it;

But beauty's waste hath in the world an end,

And kept unused, the user so destroys it.

  No love toward others in that bosom sits

  That on himself such murd'rous shame commits.

009

你是否因担心丢下遗孀泪流连连，

才以独身方式耗尽己生命的灯盏？

啊！假如你没有子嗣就溘然长逝，

世界将会像你的遗孀而失声哭泣，

像为你守寡的妻子日夜泪流不止，

只缘你身后没有留下你一丝形影。

不像别的遗孀凭借着孩子的眼睛，

将亡夫音容笑貌保存在自己心中。

瞧！世间阔绰公子哥虽挥金如土，

但只是金钱易主，他人还可享用。

而世人之美一旦浪费将一去不回，

持而不用，最终则被持有者摧毁①。

　　像这样连自己都无耻地戕害，

　　心里怎能装下对他人的怜爱？

---

① 诗人始终认为，如不结婚生子，将自己的美质遗传给后代，就是对美的浪费或摧毁。参见其十四行诗第一首、第八首、第十一首等。——译者注

010

For shame! Deny that thou bear'st love to any,

Who for thyself art so unprovident.

Grant, if thou wilt, thou art beloved of many,

But that thou none lov'st is most evident;

For thou art so possessed with murd'rous hate

That'ainst thyself thou stick'st not to conspire,

Seeking that beauteous roof to ruinate

Which to repair should be thy chief desire.

O, change thy thought, that I may change my mind!

Shall hate be fairer lodged than gentle love?

Be, as thy presence is, gracious and kind,

Or to thyself at least kind-hearted prove;

    Make thee another self, for love of me,

    That beauty still may live in thine or thee.

010

说什么你对任何人都有怜爱之心，

好不羞耻！你对自己都冷漠无情！

你应当承认有许多人对你爱意浓浓，

可毋庸置疑你对任何人无义无情。

因为在你的心中充斥着满腔怨恨，

甚至都铁了心肠设计戕害你自身。

想方设法要摧毁你那美丽的屋宇①，

而你本应该将其修缮得尽善尽美。

改弦更张吧！我会对你另眼相看。

难道怨恨比柔爱更适宜寄居你的身躯？

要像你美丽的外表，心也要美善，

或者至少对自己不再冷漠与无情。

　　你要是真的爱我，就要脱胎换骨地改变，

　　让你的美质在你或子孙身上赓续到永远。

---

① 指身体的躯壳。

011

As fast as thou shalt wane, so fast thou grow'st

In one of thine, from that which thou departest;

And that fresh blood which youngly thou bestow'st

Thou mayst call thine when thou from youth convertest.

Herein lives wisdom, beauty, and increase;

Without this, folly, age, and cold decay.

If all were minded so, the times should cease,

And threescore years would make the world away.

Let those whom Nature hath not made for store,

Harsh, featureless, and rude, barrenly perish;

Look whom she best endowed she gave the more,

Which bounteous gift thou shouldst in bounty cherish.

    She carved thee for her seal, and meant thereby

    Thou shouldst print more, not let that copy die.

011

犹如你迅速凋靡，你亦可迅速成长——
从你的后嗣身上迅速获得新生。
你年轻时所投注的新鲜血液，
即使老了也可在子嗣身上再现。
如此，智慧、美丽、繁盛赓续，
否则，愚蠢、苍老、衰靡缠身。
若人人皆持独身，时代将会终结，
只需六十载世界便彻底消夷。
让造物主使那些无意生子者
变得丑陋、野蛮，孑然死去，
而造物主宠爱的人受赐无限，
你要把这慷慨恩赐珍惜珍藏。
　　　造物主把你刻成她的印章一枚，
　　　让你不断复盖，切勿将其荒废。

012

When I do count the clock that tells the time,

And see the brave day sunk in hideous night;

When I behold the violet past prime,

And sable curls all silvered o'er with white,

When lofty trees I see barren of leaves

Which erst from heat did canopy the herd,

And summer's green all girded up in sheaves

Borne on the bier with white and bristly beard;

Then of thy beauty do I question make,

That thou among the wastes of time must go,

Since sweets and beauties do themselves forsake

And die as fast as they see others grow;

    And nothing 'gainst Time's scythe can make defense

    Save breed, to brave him when he takes thee hence.

012

当我静心细数时钟报时声声,

绚丽的白昼坠入可怕的夜空;

当我目睹那紫罗兰枯萎凋靡,

乌黑的秀发变成了银丝缕缕;

当我见到参天大树叶落纷纷,

它再也不为牧羊人避热遮阴;

曾经翠绿的夏禾扎成一捆捆

身带白色须芒,惜惜安卧在棺椁架上。

我不禁为你的美丽心生殷忧:

担心你也会没入时间的荒流,

因为美丽芬芳最终也会枯靡,

一见到新蕾萌生便迅速凋毙。

　　　世间万物都无法抵挡时间的霜刀风剑,

　　　除非你死时留下了子孙后代不绝绵延。

013

O, that you were yourself! But, love, you are

No longer yours than you yourself here live:

Against this coming end you should prepare,

And your sweet semblance to some other give.

So should that beauty which you hold in lease

Find no determination; then you were

Yourself again after yourself's decease

When your sweet issue your sweet form should bear.

Who lets so fair a house fall to decay,

Which husbandry in honor might uphold

Against the stormy gusts of winter's day

And barren rage of Death's eternal cold?

　　O, none but unthrifts! Dear my love, you know

　　You had a father; let your son say so.

013

噢，愿你永是青春无逝的自己！

可是我的爱，尘世总会让你衰靡。

你应为生命终点到来做好准备，

要把自己的靡颜腻理传给子嗣。

如此，你租赁而持有的美质

将永远不会到期，纵使你已经

离开人间，却依然如重生再世，

因为你的子嗣保留了你美丽的形质。

力尽丈夫崇高之责并潜心耕耘

以抵御严冬凛冽的狂风暴雪，

遏制冷酷死神企图绝后的妄为，

如此，还有谁能让这般美丽的殿宇崩毁？①

　　　谁也不能！除非是败家子！亲爱的，

　　　你既已然为人之子，也当为人之父②。

---

① 力尽丈夫崇高之责……美丽殿宇崩塌：诗人总认为，男人娶妻生子便可以抵御时间和大
　自然对生命的消靡，从而绵延不绝，其美貌形质——美丽的殿宇——就会长存不灭。美
　丽殿宇：喻指具美貌的形体。——译者注

② 你既已然为人之子，也当为人之父：父亲生了你，你也应当生子赓续生命。——译者注

014

Not from the stars do I my judgment pluck,

And yet methinks I have astronomy,

But not to tell of good or evil luck,

Of plagues, of dearths, or season's quality;

Nor can I fortune to brief minutes tell,

Pointing to each his thunder, rain and wind,

Or say with princes if it shall go well,

By oft predict that I in heaven find;

But from thine eyes my knowledge I derive,

And, constant stars, in them I read such art

As truth and beauty shall together thrive

If from thyself to store thou wouldst convert.

    Or else of thee this I prognosticate:

    Thy end is truth's and beauty's doom and date.

014

我从不根据星宿来做判断，

尽管我对星象并非门外汉；

我也从不用星象占卜吉凶、

饥荒、年成和瘟疫的流行；

也不预测瞬时的福祸变幻，

更不指点上苍的风雨雷电；

也不根据看到的一点天象，

妄说王公们是否飞黄腾达。

但是，我从你明亮的双眸——

这对恒星——洞悉如下真谛：

你若回心转意，娶妻生子，

真与美在你身上会同生共荣。

　　否则，我下面的预言一定成真：

　　真与美将随你人逝而剧终曲尽。

015

When I consider everything that grows

Holds in perfection but a little moment,

That this huge stage presenteth nought but shows

Whereon the stars in secret influence comment;

When I perceive that men as plants increase,

Cheerèd and checked even by the self-same sky,

Vaunt in their youthful sap, at height decrease,

And wear their brave state out of memory;

Then the conceit of this inconstant stay

Sets you most rich in youth before my sight,

Where wasteful Time debateth with Decay

To change your day of youth to sullied night;

    And, all in war with Time for love of you,

    As he takes from you, I engraft you new.

015

当我想到世间生生不息的万物，

其盛极时期也仅是短暂的一瞬，

不过是这大舞台上演的一出出活剧，

剧的优劣皆受制于星宿的神功；

当我知道人和草木一样繁衍生息，

都受同一上苍的约束与激励，

且少时心浮气盛，盛过则朝气衰靡，

往昔的飒爽英姿成为了依稀记忆，

这种人生无常变幻常令我陷入沉思，

你年少时的勃勃雄姿浮现在我的眼前，

时间暴君与夺春鬼相互争辩，

如何把你青春的白昼①变成肮脏的暗夜②。

　　为了爱你，我要尽全力与时间暴君抗争，

　　它要夺你的青春，我则嫁嫩芽让你新生。

---

① 青春的白昼：指风华正茂的青年时期。——译者注

② 暗夜：喻指人的暮年。——译者注

016

But wherefore do not you a mightier way

Make war upon this bloody tyrant, Time?

And fortify yourself in your decay

With means more blessèd than my barren rime?

Now stand you on the top of happy hours,

And many maiden gardens, yet unset,

With virtuous wish would bear your living flowers,

Much liker than your painted counterfeit.

So should the lines of life that life repair

Which this time's pencil or my pupil pen,

Neither in inward worth nor outward fair

Can make you live yourself in eyes of men.

　　　To give away yourself keeps yourself still,

　　　And you must live, drawn by your own sweet skill.

016

你为何不用更强力的手段，

与这血腥的时间暴君宣战，

或用比吾诗更神圣的方式，

来拯救你不断逝去的芳年？

现如今你已站在幸时之巅，

有许多尚未开垦的处女园，

期待着为你开出芳花朵朵①，

而且比你的画像更像你的容颜。

生命只能靠生命延绵赓续，

拙笔与时间画匠都无能为力

把你内在之美和外在之丽

画得像世人眼中看到的你。

　　　　只有生子为父，你才能让自己弥久赓续，

　　　　自己的生命之画，要靠自己精湛的画技。

---

① 芳花朵朵：喻指子孙后代。——译者注

017

Who will believe my verse in time to come

If it were filled with your most high deserts?

Though yet, heaven knows, it is but as a tomb

Which hides your life and shows not half your parts.

If I could write the beauty of your eyes

And in fresh numbers number all your graces,

The age to come would say, "This poet lies —

Such heavenly touches ne'er touched earthly faces."

So should my papers, yellowed with their age,

Be scorned, like old men of less truth than tongue,

And your true rights be termed a poet's rage

And stretchèd metre of an antique song.

　　But were some child of yours alive that time,

　　You should live twice, in it and in my rime.

017

将来有谁会相信我的诗章，
即使通篇都是对你的赞扬。
上苍虽知这不过是一座坟冢
隐藏你的一生，难显你英名。
纵然我能写出你眼睛美丽，
用清新的诗行写尽你芳容，
将来有人会说"这诗尽是谎言；
这天上才有的美貌怎会落在人间？"
于是我那泛黄的陈年诗稿，
被当做饶舌的老叟受嘲笑。
你应得之赞被说成我的狂想——
一首矫揉造作的陈腐诗章。
　　但是，如果你有子孙活在那个时期，
　　你将同时活在他们身上和我的诗里。

018

Shall I compare thee to a summer's day?

Thou art more lovely and more temperate.

Rough winds do shake the darling buds of May,

And summer's lease hath all too short a date.

Sometime too hot the eye of heaven shines,

And often is his gold complexion dimmed;

And every fair from fair sometime declines,

By chance or nature's changing course untrimmed:

But thy eternal summer shall not fade

Nor lose possession of that fair thou ow'st;

Nor shall Death brag thou wand'rest in his shade

When in eternal lines to time thou grow'st.

  So long as men can breathe or eyes can see,

  So long lives this, and this gives life to thee.

018

我可否把你比作夏日绮丽？

其实你比夏日更温柔娇眹。

狂风恣肆摧残五月的花蕾，

夏日时光短暂会匆匆离去；

苍天眸子①常使人灼热难御，

它金色的面庞时常被阴翳。

夏日的群芳百媚也会衰替，

或因偶然或因时变而枯毙。

唯你绵亘的夏日永不逝去，

你天生的质丽也永不凋靡。

死神也难让你行游其辖域，

你将伴随这诗章千古不息。

　　只要人类双目不瞑，呼吸不止，

　　这诗将长存，亦使你流芳百世！

---

① 苍天眸子：喻指太阳。——译者注

019

Devouring time, blunt thou the lion's paws,

And make the earth devour her own sweet brood;

Pluck the keen teeth from the fierce tiger's jaws,

And burn the long-lived phoenix in her blood;

Make glad and sorry seasons as they fleet'st,

And do whate'er thou wilt, swift-footed Time,

To the wide world and all her fading sweets,

But I forbid thee one most heinous crime:

O, carve not with thy hours my love's fair brow,

Nor draw no lines there with thine antique pen;

Him in thy course untainted do allow

For beauty's pattern to succeeding men.

  Yet, do thy worst, old Time: despite thy wrong,

  My love shall in my verse ever live young.

019

贪婪的时间暴君你磨钝了狮爪，

让大地吞噬它自己可爱的幼崽。

你从猛虎口中拔出其利齿，

把长生的凤凰在血泊中烧成灰烬。

让四季随你的飞逝悲喜交错，

如梭的时光，任凭你为所欲为，

横扫广袤旷野，千芳百花残，

但有一桩重罪绝不允许你犯：

切勿用时光之刀残刻吾爱美丽的容颜，

也不能用你陈腐的画笔在他脸上胡涂乱画，

要让他在你时光征途上一尘不染，

为后世的人们留下美的光辉典范。

　　不过，时间老君！尽管你横施暴虐，

　　吾爱依然会在我的诗章里青春永驻。

020

A woman's face, with Nature's own hand painted,

Hast thou, the master-mistress of my passion;

A woman's gentle heart, but not acquainted

With shifting change, as is false women's fashion;

An eye more bright than theirs, less false in rolling,

Gilding the object whereupon it gazeth;

A man in hue, all hues in his controlling,

Which steals men's eyes and women's souls amazeth.

And for a woman wert thou first created,

Till Nature, as she wrought thee, fell a-doting,

And by addition me of thee defeated,

By adding one thing to my purpose nothing.

    But since she pricked thee out for women's pleasure,

    Mine be thy love, and thy love's use their treasure.

020

造物主亲手绘就你那女人般的面庞，

你既是我的情妇，又是我的情郎。

你的内心充满着女人的纤纤柔情，

却无女人的轻佻善变和造作虚荣。

你的眼睛比女人的明亮而不轻浮，

你目光所落之处，顿生熠熠金辉。

一身男人的风采令所有风采披靡，

勾去男人的眼神，掠走女人的芳魂。

造物主最初本将你制成红颜佳丽，

怎奈在施工中却因你而落魄失神，

把一件对我无用的东西加在你身，

从而剥夺了我承欢于你的一腔深情。

　　既然她造你完全是为了女人欢娱，

　　那你就把心爱给我，把身爱给她们。

021

So is it not with me as with that Muse,

Stirred by a painted beauty to his verse,

Who heaven itself for ornament doth use

And every fair with his fair doth rehearse,

Making a couplement of proud compare

With sun and moon, with earth and sea's rich gems,

With April's first-born flowers, and all things rare

That heaven's airs in this huge rondure hems.

O, let me, true in love, but truly write,

And then believe me, my love is as fair

As any mother's child, though not so bright

As those gold candles fixed in heaven's air.

    Let them say more that like of hearsay well;

    I will not praise that purpose not to sell.

021

我与那位诗人君完全不同，

他一见粉黛便会诗情骚动。

甚至把苍天用来赞美他的美人，

极尽美辞把佳丽赞颂。

堆砌各种虚华辞藻来打比方：

什么日月大地，海中珍稀，

什么四月初绽的花朵，

乃至漭弥苍穹下一切奇珍。

而我则真诚地爱，真实地写，

噢！请大家一定要相信我，

吾爱美如母亲怀中的赤子，

虽不如苍穹中的金烛①明亮。

　　　让那些诗人用华丽辞藻虚夸吧，

　　　我并非为兜售，也就无须夸口。

---

① 金烛：指星星。——译者注

022

My glass shall not persuade me I am old

So long as youth and thou are of one date;

But when in thee time's furrows I behold,

Then look I death my days should expiate.

For all that beauty that doth cover thee

Is but the seemly raiment of my heart,

Which in thy breast doth live, as thine in me.

How can I then be elder than thou art?

O, therefore, love, be of thyself so wary

As I, not for myself, but for thee will;

Bearing thy heart, which I will keep so chary

As tender nurse her babe from faring ill.

>Presume not on thy heart when mine is slain;

>Thou gav'st me thine not to give back again.

022

只要你总是与青春相伴相随，
镜子休想让我相信我人已衰微。
但是看到你脸上的时光刻痕，
感到我岁月的终点即将来临。
因为包裹你全身的美丽外表，
就像罩在我内心的可身的衣衫。
你与我心连着心，心心相印，
因此，我岂能比你先转衰变老？
噢，我的爱，你要保重身体，
如同我为你而非为我珍重我自己。
我心承着你心，我会倍加珍惜，
犹如慈母怕婴儿染病而精心护理。

　　如若我心已先碎，你切莫将你心收回，
　　你既已把心给我，我不会再奉还给你。

023

As an unperfect actor on the stage

Who with his fear is put besides his part,

Or some fierce thing replete with too much rage,

Whose strength's abundance weakens his own heart;

So I, for fear of trust, forget to say

The perfect ceremony of love's rite,

And in mine own love's strength seem to decay,

O'ercharged with burthen of mine own love's might.

O, let my books be then the eloquence

And dump presagers of my speaking breast,

Who plead for love and look for recompense,

More than that tongue that more hath more expressed.

O, learn to read what silent love hath writ;

To hear with eyes belongs to love's fine wit.

023

像一名尚未成熟的戏剧演员，

因紧张一上场把台词全忘记；

或者像一头狂暴至极的猛兽，

浑身是力反倒使其内心恐惧。

我就是因为紧张、缺少自信，

该对爱人郑重表白时却蓦然语塞；

心中爱之强烈犹如负重千钧，

反使爱的热烈的激情似乎消靡。

噢，那就让我的诗章去表白吧！

让这无声使者吐露我一腔深情；

让它替我表白，找回我的爱，

它将胜过聒噪之舌而娓娓道来。

　　噢，要学会阅读用无声的爱写成的诗章，

　　学会用眼睛"聆听"爱之精妙绝伦的表白。

024

Mine eye hath played the painter and hath stelled

Thy beauty's form in table of my heart;

My body is the frame wherein'tis held,

And perspective it is best painter's art.

For through the painter must you see his skill

To find where your true image pictured lies,

Which in my bosom's shop is hanging still,

That hath his windows glazèd with thine eyes.

Now see what good turns eyes for eyes have done:

Mine eyes have drawn thy shape, and thine for me

Are windows to my breast, wherethrough the sun

Delights to peep, to gaze therein on thee.

     Yet eyes this cunning want to grace their art;

     They draw but what they see, know not the heart.

024

我的眼睛扮演着一位画家，

将你的美貌画在我的心田。

我的身躯是装裱它的画框，

透视法是画家惯用的技法；

你要透过画家看他的画技，

才能找到何处是画像的真谛。

这画一直挂在我内心的画廊，

你明亮的眼睛就是画廊的窗扉。

我们相对而视，深情凝望：

我的眼睛画出你美丽的形体，

你的明眸成了洞悉我心灵的绮窗，

太阳透过这窗扉欣喜地把你窥视和凝望。

　　可是我的眼睛还没有入木三分的精湛画技，

　　只能画所见其人之表，不能洞悉其人之心。

025

Let those who are in favor with their stars

Of public honor and proud titles boast,

Whilst I, whom fortune of such triumph bars,

Unlooked for joy in that I honor most.

Great princes' favorites their fair leaves spread

But as the marigold at the sun's eye;

And in themselves their pride lies burièd,

For at a frown they in their glory die.

The painful warrior famousèd for fight,

After a thousand victories once foiled,

Is from the book of honor rasèd quite,

And all the rest forgot for which he toiled.

> Then happy I, that love and am beloved

> Where I may not remove nor be removed.

025

且让那些吉星高照的人们夸耀吧，
夸耀他们地位显赫和功名卓著！
而我命中与这些殊荣无缘，
却意外地找到了我心中的最爱。
朝廷重臣虽能一时风光显赫，
却像阳光照耀下的金盏花，
其绚烂的风采最终会凋靡，
龙颜一怒他们便荣光全无。
沙场上拼死取得的赫赫战功
换来的荣誉，却因一朝失利
便从功劳簿上一笔勾销，
即便功高盖世也无人再记起。
　　故而庆幸自己幸福萦绕，真爱相随，
　　无须看人脸色，无须担心官场失意。

026

Lord of my love, to whom in vassalage

Thy merit hath my duty strongly knit,

To thee I send this written ambassage

To witness duty, not to show my wit.

Duty so great, which wit so poor as mine

May make seem bare, in wanting words to show it,

But that I hope some good coneit of thine

In thy soul's thought, all naked, will bestow it,

Till whatsoever star that guides my moving

Points on me graciously with fair aspect,

And puts apparel on my tattered loving

To show me worthy of thy sweet respect.

     Then may I dare to boast how I do love thee,

     Till then not show my head where thou mayest prove me.

026

我的爱，我至高至尊的阁下，

你的美德俘获了我的耿耿忠心。

兹向阁下奉上我的拙诗一首，

旨在向您献忠心而非炫文采。

我虽才疏学浅，但忠心无限，

贫乏的语汇或难以将忠心尽表，

但我期冀你用深邃的洞察力

明鉴这颗赤诚的心并予晒纳。

待我鸿运当头，高照的吉星

指引我前行迈向似锦前程之时，

请你也为我褴褛的爱换上锦衣，

以便配得上接受阁下的恩惠。

　　到那时我才敢夸口说我是多么爱你无限，

　　而在此之前我怎敢见你，接受你的考验？

027

Weary with toil, I haste me to my bed,

The dear repose for limbs with travel tir'd,

But then begins a journey in my head

To work my mind when body's work's expir'd;

For then my thoughts, from far where I abide,

Intend a zealous pilgrimage to thee,

And keep my drooping eyelids open wide,

Looking on darkness which the blind do see;

Save that my soul's imaginary sight

Presents thy shadow to my sightless view,

Which, like a jewel hung in ghastly night,

Makes black night beauteous and her old face new.

  Lo, thus, by day my limbs, by night my mind,

  For thee and for myself no quiet find.

027

我因精疲力竭匆匆地去入睡，

让旅途劳顿的身躯得以安歇。

但此时脑海里的旅行再次开始，

躯体在安歇，而心灵在劳累。

我的思绪从远方飞到你身边，

对你奉上最热忱虔诚的朝拜。

我倾力睁大惺忪困顿的双眼，

如同盲人"所见"，一片漆黑。

但是，我那灵魂想象的双眸，

把你的倩影呈现在漆黑的眼前，

像一颗宝石高悬在茫茫夜空，

顿时一片明亮，让夜空金光闪闪。

　　瞧！白天我的身驰，夜晚我的心骋，

　　为你，也为我，得不到片刻的安宁。

028

How can I then return in happy plight

That am debarr'd the benefit of rest,

When day's oppression is not eas'd by night,

But day by night, and night by day, oppressed

And each, though enemies to either's reign,

Do in consent shake hands to torture me,

The one by toil, the other to complain

How far I toil, still farther off from thee?

I tell the day, to please him, thou art bright

And dost him grace when clouds do blot the heaven;

So flatter I the swart-complexioned night,

When sparkling stars twire not, thou gild'st the even.

> But day doth daily draw my sorrows longer,
>
> And night doth nightly make grief's strength seem
>
> stronger.

028

就连休息的权益都被剥夺，

白天劳累夜晚都无法解脱，

因而受着日夜的双重压迫，

那我怎能恢复心境的快乐？

尽管白昼与黑夜本是敌人，

但为了折磨我却握手言和；

我白天受劳役，夜晚陷哀愁：

离你如此遥远，寻你不知还走多久？

我讨好白天说你光芒四射，

乌云遮日时你能让其明澈；

讨好夜晚说能熠熠生辉，

星星不亮时你能照亮暗夜。

　　　可是白昼令我日陷深愁，

　　　夜晚却更让我愁上加愁。

029

When, in disgrace with Fortune and men's eyes,

I all alone beweep my outcast state,

And trouble deaf heaven with my bootless cries,

And look upon myself and curse my fate,

Wishing me like to one more rich in hope,

Featured like him, like him with friend's possess'd,

Desiring this man's art, and that man's scope,

With what I most enjoy contented least;

Yet in these thoughts myself almost despising,

Haply I think on thee, and then my state,

Like to the lark at break of day arising

From sullen earth, sings hymns at heaven's gate;

    For thy sweet love remember'd such wealth brings

    That then I scorn to change my state with kings.

029

面对背运煎熬和众人的白眼，

只能孤独地哀叹自己的落寞，

对聋聩的苍天哀嚎无济于事，

只有自我反思诅咒命运不济。

徒愿自己能像人家那样前途无量，

像此君那样美貌盖世无双，仰慕者满堂，

像彼君那样才华横溢，锦绣前程，

而自己醉心的事却相形见绌①；

这妄自菲薄的思绪挥之不去，

却猛然间想到了你，顿感幸福至极，

像黎明一只振翅高飞的云雀，

从茫茫大地飞到浩瀚天宇，放声高歌。

　　　　你甘美的爱是无价财宝，我紧紧扼守于心田，

　　　　就算是王公贵族的爵位，我也不屑与其交换。

---

① 诗人不仅出身低微，而且未受过高等教育，从文法学校毕业后便当了演员并开始了写剧
本，后来虽小有名气，但在当时仍无社会地位。自己醉心的事：即诗人喜欢的演艺事业
和戏剧创作。——译者注

030

When to the sessions of sweet silent thought

I summon up remembrance of things past,

I sigh the lack of many a thing I sought,

And with old woes new wail my dear time's waste.

Then can I drown an eye, unus'd to flow,

For precious friends hid in death's dateless night,

And weep afresh love's long since cancell'd woe,

And moan th' expense of many a vanish'd sight.

Then can I grieve at grievances foregone,

And heavily from woe to woe tell o'er

The sad account of fore-bemoanèd moan,

Which I new pay as if not paid before.

      But if the while I think on thee, dear friend,

      All losses are restored and sorrows end.

030

当我陷入甜美的沉思默想，
总唤起对往昔的追忆与回望，
慨叹许多事情未如愿以偿，
痛惜往日失去的美好时光。
从不轻弹的热泪潸然流淌，
既为永眠在长夜的挚友哀伤，
也叹息众多往事如云烟飘茫，
还勾起我心藏已久的情殇。
如今依然因往事心怀惆怅，
缕缕愁绪萦绕在我的心房，
昔日的悲伤已成陈年积账，
如今仿佛将旧债彻底清偿。

　　亲爱的朋友，每当想起你，
　　所失皆回归，愁云尽消靡。

031

Thy bosom is endearèd with all hearts

Which I by lacking have supposèd dead;

And their reigns love and all love's loving parts,

And all those friends which I thought burièd.

How many a holy and obsequious tear

Hath dear religious love stol'n from mine eye,

As interest of the dead, which now appear

But things removed that hidden in thee lie!

Thou art the grave where buried love doth live,

Hung with the trophies of my lovers gone,

Who all their parts of me to thee did give;

That due of many now is thine alone.

    Their images I lov'd I vew in thee,

    And thou, all they, hast all the all of me.

031

多少颗挚爱的心^①本以为已消逝，

原来全都珍藏在了你的心里；

多少长眠的朋友本以为已埋葬，

原来都去沐浴你的爱和爱之光；

多少为逝者潸然而下的圣洁泪珠，

把我至真的爱从眼里悄悄偷走。

现在看来，那些与世长辞的亡友

原来只是迁徙，安藏在了你心里！

你是爱的墓冢，爱虽葬犹生，

冢里挂满亡友的徽章勾起故情深深。

他们把我的一腔深情都献给了你，

本该许多人共享的爱却唯你独享。

　　我在你身上看到了吾爱的身影；

　　你就是他们全体——我所有的爱——却都由你占有。

---

① 心：替代用法，指挚爱的友人。——译者注

032

If thou survive my well-contented day

When that churl Death my bones with dust shall cover,

And shalt by fortune once more resurvey

These poor rude lines of thy deceasèd lover,

Compare them with the bettering of the time,

And though they be outstripped by every pen,

Reserve them for my love, not for their rime,

Exceeded by the height of happier men.

O, then vouchsafe me but this loving thought:

"Had my friend's Muse grown with this growing age,

A dearer birth than this his love had brought

To march in ranks of better equipage;

    But since he died, and poets better prove,

    Theirs for their style I'll read, his for his love."

032

假如我驾鹤西去你依然在世，

在死神把我埋葬于黄泉以后，

你若偶然看到你亡友曾写的拙诗，

纵使与后世才俊的妙文相比，

不及它们异彩纷呈，

为了我的爱而非为拙诗本身，

一定要将这些陋作残稿保存，

尽管它们不及时运宠儿的雄文。

那时你要对我抱有这样的爱意：

"假如吾友诗才可与时俱进，

他的爱能让更美的诗章问世，

可与当世的才俊们一起同领风骚。

　　但他英年早逝，而后世诗才却诗艺徒升，

　　我品赏后世的文采，而感悟吾友的挚爱。"

033

Full many a glorious morning have I seen

Flatter the mountain tops with sovereign eye,

Kissing with golden face the meadows green,

Gilding pale streams with heavenly alchemy;

Anon permit the basest clouds to ride

With ugly rack on his celestial face,

And from the forlorn world his visage hide,

Stealing unseen to west with this disgrace.

Even so my sun one early morn did shine

With all-triumphant splendor on my brow;

But, out alack! He was but one hour mine,

The region cloud hath masked him from me now.

　　　Yet him for this my love no whit disdaineth;

　　　Suns of the world may stain when heaven's sun staineth.

033

在无数个明媚和煦的清晨，

我看到灿烂朝阳抚慰着山峦，

用他金色面庞亲吻绿色草原，

用点金术让苍白溪水变得金光灿烂；

可是蓦然又让乌云遮天，

被丑陋的云翳遮住了他精美绝伦的脸庞，

令茫茫世界见不到他的容颜，

风范不再，悄悄地溜向西天的地平线。

我的朝阳也曾在清晨闪耀，

将璀璨的光芒洒在我眉间。

可惜他属于我的时间太短；

今天，乌云①已把我和他隔断。

　　可是，我对他的爱丝毫不减，

　　尽管日神会变暗、世情会变淡。

① 这里"乌云"是虚指，指诗人与其所爱的人之间的障碍。——译者注

034

Why didst thou promise such a beauteous day

And make me travel forth without my cloak,

To let base clouds o'ertake me in my way,

Hiding thy brav'ry in their rotten smoke?

'Tis not enough that through the cloud thou break

To dry the rain on my storm-beaten face,

For no man well of such a salve can speak

That heals the wound, and cures not the disgrace:

Nor can thy shame give physic to my grief;

Though thou repent, yet I have still the loss:

Th' offender's sorrow lends but weak relief

To him that bears the strong offense's cross.

    Ah, but those tears are pearl which thy love sheeds,

    And they are rich and ransom all ill deeds.

034

你为什么许给我一个晴空丽日？

害得我没带雨衣就匆匆上路，

让卑鄙的云雨路上对我袭击，

阴霾也让你灿烂的光辉蓦然消逝。

现在你即使拨开了密布的乌云，

也难晒干我被雨打湿的脸颊，

没人会称赞这种治病药方，

因为它只治外伤，不医受伤的自尊心，

你的愧疚无法医治我内心的痛楚，

你虽已后悔，但我依然伤心，

伤害了别人，无论怎么自责，

也难驱除受害者内心的伤痕。

　　　不过，你用爱洒下的滴滴眼泪赛若珍珠，

　　　它们弥足珍贵，足以把你的恶行救赎。

035

No more be grieved at that which thou hast done:

Roses have thorns, and silver fountains mud;

Clouds and eclipses stain both moon and sun,

And loathsome canker lives in sweetest bud.

All men make faults, and even I in this,

Authorizing thy trespass with compare,

Myself corrupting, salving thy amiss,

Excusing thy sins more than thy sins are.

For to thy sensual fault I bring in sense —

Thy adverse party is thy advocate —

And 'gainst myself a lawful plea commence;

Such civil war is in my love and hate

    That I an accessory needs must be

    To that sweet thief which sourly robs from me.

035

切莫再为你的过失而悲伤；

玫瑰有刺，清泉有时也溷泥，

日尚有云翳，月亦有圆缺，

美丽的花蕾有时把害虫藏。

人无完人，我也难免犯错，

用这些比喻是为你的罪责开脱——

贬低自己，掩饰你的罪过。

而原谅你的罪过比你的罪过还罪不可赦。

我为了掩饰你的放荡不羁，

却由对手变成了你的辩护人，

甚至对自己提起诉讼——

内心充斥着一场爱憎之间的激烈斗争，

　　　以至于我不得不沦为你的同谋，

　　　帮你这个温柔的小偷对我自己行窃。

036

Let me confess that we two must be twain

Although our undivided loves are one:

So shall those blots that do with me remain,

Without thy help, by me be borne alone.

In our two loves there is but one respect,

Though in our lives a separable spite,

Which though it alter not love's sole effect,

Yet doth it steal sweet hours from love's delight.

I may not evermore acknowledge thee,

Lest my bewailèd guilt should do thee shame;

Nor thou with public kindness honor me

Unless thou take that honor from thy name,

    But do not so; I love thee in such sort

    As, thou being mine, mine is thy good report.

036

我得承认我们俩必须分手，

尽管我们的爱融为一体而牢不可破。

如此，我的污垢都留给自己，

我的玷辱无需你来背负；

这样我们的爱一同受人尊重，

尽管两个生命各有各的烦忧。

分离虽不能改变挚爱至真，

但会失去许多爱的欢乐时光。

我不再当众认你为知己，

以免我可悲的罪过让你蒙羞。

你也不要再当众对我抬爱，

除非你甘愿让你的英名受辱。

　　切莫！因为我是如此地爱你，

　　你属于我，我也要为你增辉。

037

As a decrepit father takes delight

To see his active child do deeds of youth,

So I, made lame by Fortune's dearest spite,

Take all my comfort of thy worth and truth.

For whether beauty, birth, or wealth, or wit,

Or any of these all, or all, or more,

Intitled in thy parts to crownèd sit,

I make my love ingrafted to this store.

So then I am not lame, poor, nor despis'd

Whilst that this shadow doth such substance give

That I in thy abundance am suffic'd

And by a part of all thy glory live.

      Look, what is best, that best I wish in thee.

      This wish I have; then ten times happy me!

037

像衰微的父亲一样心怀良愿，

巴望着孩子趁年轻就卓越超凡。

我虽然被命运不济深深困羁，

却因为你的美德和挚诚而备感慰藉。

在你身上所具有的全部美质——

貌美质丽和高贵出身都举世无双，

财富和智慧也无人能与你比肩。

我把我的爱嫁接于你这些美质，

便不再被困境、贫穷、鄙视所烦扰。

既然把缥缈的幻影变为了现实，

我在你的富足中也变得充盈，

借你一份荣光而获得新生。

　　愿世间至美至珍都集于你一身，

　　我将感到幸福无比，夙愿终成真！

038

How can my Muse want subject to invent

While thou dost breathe, that pour'st into my verse

Thine own sweet argument, too excellent

For every vulgar paper to rehearse?

O, give thyself the thanks, if aught in me

Worthy perusal stand against thy sight,

For who's so dumb that cannot write to thee,

When thou thyself dost give invention light?

Be thou the tenth Muse, ten times more in worth

Than those old nine which rimers invocate;

And he that calls on thee, let him bring forth

Eternal numbers to outlive long date.

    If my slight Muse do please these curious days,

    The pain be mine, but thine shall be the praise.

038

我的诗神怎会缺少诗心和诗情?

你吐一口气,我就会大发诗兴,

把你美妙的意趣注入我的诗行,

如此美妙,庸俗诗人怎能吟诵?

你若在我的诗里看到妙语佳句,

噢!那还得感谢你诗神自己!

当你为诗人注入了写诗的灵感,

他怎会木讷到不为你写诗赞美?

做第十位缪斯吧!你远胜过

诗人们以往祈求的那九位诗神十倍。

对于虔诚地祈求你的这位诗人①

让他思如泉涌,写出不朽诗文!

　　如果我浅疏的诗才可让这个苛求的时代满意,

　　那辛苦执笔的是我,而该受赞扬的应是你。

---

① 这里指诗人自己。——译者注

039

O, how thy worth with manners may I sing

When thou art all the better part of me?

What can mine own praise to mine own self bring?

And what is't but mine own when I praise thee?

Even for this let us divided live

And our dear love lose name of single one,

That by this separation I may give

That due to thee which thou deserv'st alone.

O absence, what a torment wouldst thou prove

Were it not thy sour leisure gave sweet leave

To entertain the time with thoughts of love,

Which time and thoughts so sweetly doth deceive,

    And that thou teachest how to make one twain,

    By praising him here who doth hence remain!

039

我该如何恰如其分地把你赞颂，

如果你胜过我而又与我共为一体？

赞美你时又岂不是也在赞美我自己？

而自己赞美自己又有何旨趣？

为此，我们两人应独处别离，

让我俩之间的挚爱不再共享同一名义；

一旦分别，我便可悉数奉还

你本应独享的所有荣誉。

噢，别离啊！要不是你用枯燥的闲暇让我得以甜蜜独处，

使我沉浸在充满爱的情思的时光里

甜美地怡享时光和情思惜惜流逝；

要不是你教会我如何化形单为影双，

　　　　使我可以在此对远别的吾爱倾情赞扬①，

　　　　不然，那将会使我忍受何等的愁伤！

---

① 如本诗开头所述，他与其爱共为一体时，顾忌"赞美你时又岂不是也在赞美自己"，现在一经分开，便可无所顾忌地对其爱倾情赞扬。——译者注

040

Take all my loves, my love, yea, take them all;

What hast thou then more than thou hadst before?

No love, my love, that thou mayst true love call;

All mine was thine before thou hadst this more.

Then if for my love thou my love receivest,

I cannot blame thee for my love thou usest;

But yet be blamed if thou this self deceivest

By wilful taste of what thyself refusest.

I do forgive thy robb'ry, gentle thief,

Although thou steal thee all my poverty;

And yet love knows it is a greater grief

To bear love's wrong than hate's known injury.

  Lascivious grace, in whom all ill well shows,

  Kill me with spites; yet we must not be foes.

040

要夺走我所有的爱，那就拿去吧！

看看与你已有的爱相比多了多少？

我的爱啊，没有真情，遑谈真爱？

我的一切早就属于你，还夺什么？

你要是为爱我而夺走我所爱，

我不会因你与其欢爱而怪你。

但你若只是贪尝无情之欲，

自欺欺人，理应受到责怪。

我饶恕你这个温柔的偷情汉，

尽管你把我仅存的东西都偷走。

爱心懂得，失爱令人痛不欲生，

而承受失爱之痛远超仇恨之伤。

　　风流之韵，其劣行也尽显风流，

　　你可对我恨之入骨，但我不会与你结怨记仇。

041

Those petty wrongs that liberty commits,

When I am sometime absent from thy heart,

Thy beauty and thy years full well befits,

For still temptation follows where thou art.

Gentle thou art and therefore to be won,

Beauteous thou art, therefore to be assailed;

And when a woman woos, what woman's son

Will sourly leave her till she have prevailed?

Ay me! but yet thou mightest my seat forbear,

And chide try beauty and thy straying youth,

Who lead thee in their riot even there

Where thou art forced to break a twofold truth,

    Hers, by thy beauty tempting her to thee,

    Thine, by thy beauty being false to me.

041

趁我有时对你稍不留意，

你便放荡不羁，纵情风流。

这是因你貌美和年轻使然，

到哪儿都泛起诱惑的波澜。

你温柔高贵，当赢得芳心，

你貌美优雅，当爱慕者成群。

当一个女人向一个男人求欢，

哪个男人会忍心离去不让她梦圆？

可是呀，你怎么能夺我之欢！？

都怪你的美貌和放浪的青春，

诱使你放浪形骸、偷香窃玉，

最终让你被迫毁掉双重荣誉：

  毁她之荣，因你的美貌使她失身于你，

  毁你之誉，你因美貌而对我不忠不义。

042

That thou hast her, it is not all my grief,

And yet it may be said I lov'd her dearly;

That she hath thee, is of my wailing chief,

A loss in love that touches me more nearly.

Loving offenders, thus I will excuse ye:

Thou dost love her, because thou know'st I love her;

And for my sake even so doth she abuse me,

Suffering my friend for my sake to approve her.

If I lose thee, my loss is my love's gain,

And, losing her, my friend hath found that loss;

Both find each other, and I lose both twain,

And both for my sake lay on me this cross,

But here's the joy; my friend and I are one;

Sweet flattery! Then she loves but me alone.

042

我并不因你夺走了她悲痛万分，

虽然可以说我曾对她一往情深。

她对你情意缠绵才让我痛不欲生，

最深的伤害莫过于失去爱情。

"爱情的罪人"哟，我来为你们开脱吧：

你爱她，是因为你知道我爱她，

她骗我，初衷也完全是为了我，

因而才有劳吾友替我续云雨之情。

我若失去你，我所失即她所得，

我若失去她，我所失即你所获，

你们相互缠绵，我则失去你二人，

你们为了我，才让我受尽煎熬。

　　　我索性苦中作乐：既然你和我是一体，

　　　那她爱的正是我自己——多妙的自我慰藉！

043

When most I wink, then do mine eyes best see,

For all the day they view things unrespected;

But when I sleep, in dreams they look on thee,

And, darkly bright, are bright in dark directed.

Then thou, whose shadow shadows doth make bright,

How would thy shadow's form form happy show

To the clear day with thy much clearer light,

When to unseeing eyes thy shade shines so!

How would, I say, mine eyes be blessed made

By looking on thee in the living day,

When in dead night thy fair imperfect shade

Through heavy sleep on sightless eyes doth stay!

　　All days are nights to see till I see thee,

　　And nights bright days when dreams do show thee me.

043

我眼睛闭得愈紧，看得就愈清，

它们白天所见皆平淡无奇，

当我入睡后，梦中看到你，

它们在黑夜愈发明澈，目光投向你明亮的倩影——

你的倩影给黑暗带来了光明。

既然你的身影暗夜都能照亮，

何不用你更灿烂的光辉让玉宇清澄，

造出一道更加令人愉悦的风景！

既然我在漆黑的夜晚透过紧闭的双眼

在睡梦中能感受到你隐约而动的倩影，

那么，在生机勃勃的白天看到你，

我的双眼一定能感到幸福无比！

　　　看不到你，所有白天都是暗夜漆黑一片，

　　　梦里看见你，所有黑夜都是明媚的白天。

044

If the dull substance of my flesh were thought,

Injurious distance should not stop my way;

For then, despite of space, I would be brought

From limits far remote where thou dost stay.

No matter then, although my foot did stand

Upon the farthest earth removed from thee;

For nimble thought can jump both sea and land

As soon as think the place where he would be.

But ah! Thought kills me that I am not thought,

To leap large lengths of miles when thou art gone,

But that, so much of earth and water wrought,

I must attend time's leisure with my moan,

     Receiving nought by elements so slow

     But heavy tears, badges of either's woe.

044

假如我这笨重的肉体是灵动的思维，
群山万壑也挡不住我前进的步履。
虽然路途遥遥，征途漫漫，
即使你在天涯海角我也要到你身边。
纵使与你相隔千山万水，
之于我那又有何妨？
灵动的思维能漂洋过海，
想去哪里就无往而不至。
可是啊，我不是灵动的思维，只是日夜渴望，
却不能穿越过关山迢递沿着你离去时的足迹追寻你，
而我是土和水做成的肉身，
只能哀叹声声陪伴流逝的光阴。

  两种元素如此迟钝，怎能生出灵动思维，
   只有这如雨泪水诉说我心头的无限愁绪。

045

The other two, slight air and purging fire,

Are both with thee, wherever I abide;

The first my thought, the other my desire,

These present-absent with swift motion slide.

For when these quicker elements are gone

In tender embassy of love to thee,

My life, being made of four, with two alone

Sinks down to death, oppress'd with melancholy;

Until life's composition be recur'd

By those swift messengers return'd from thee,

Who even but now come back again, assur'd

Of thy fair health, recounting it to me.

    This told, I joy; but then no longer glad,

    I send them back again and straight grow sad.

045

我生命还有两种元素：轻风和净火，
任我到哪里，它们与我都形影相随。
轻风是我的思想，净火是我的愿望，
它们出没无常，总是行踪飘茫。
这两种元素轻快敏捷，离开我时，
作为使者把我温情挚爱带给你，
由四大元素构成的生命现在只剩下土和水，
怀着一腔愁绪向死亡深渊坠去；
除非两位使者从你身边返回，
才能让我生命组成重新规复。
此时恰逢两位使者再次归来，
向我报告你贵体安康无恙。

　　我闻讯大喜，可惜喜未久留，
　　我再次将两位使者遣回，却又深陷忧愁。

046

Mine eye and heart are at a mortal war,

How to divide the conquest of thy sight;

Mine eye my heart thy picture's sight would bar,

My heart mine eye the freedom of that right.

My heart doth plead that thou in him dost lie —

A closet never pierc'd with crystal eyes —

But the defendant doth that plea deny

And says in him thy fair appearance lies.

To 'cide this title is impannelèd

A quest of thoughts, all tenants to the heart,

And by their verdict is determinèd

The clear eye's moiety and the dear heart's part:

  As thus; mine eye's due is thy outward part,

  And my heart's right thy inward love of heart.

046

我的眼睛和心灵正陷入一场纷争：

如何分配战利品——你的芳容。

眼睛阻止心灵分享你的倩影；

心灵不许眼睛自由地欣赏你的姣容，

声称你原本就寄居在它的殿宇——

一双明眸看不到的幽居。

而眼睛对此矢口否认，

声称你的芳容就寓居在它们的瑶池。

判定你的芳容归属应迅速决断，

只好求助思想——心灵的房客

组成陪审团做出公正判决，

结果裁定明眸和柔心各得其所：

　　　你外在的美归我的眼睛，

　　　你内心的情归我的心灵。

047

Betwixt mine eye and heart a league is took,

And each doth good turns now unto the other:

When that mine eye is famish'd for a look,

Or heart in love with sighs himself doth smother,

With my love's picture then my eye doth feast

And to the painted banquet bids my heart;

Another time mine eye is my heart's guest

And in his thoughts of love doth share a part:

So, either by thy picture or my love,

Thyself, away, art resent still with me;

For thou not farther than my thoughts canst move,

And I am still with them and they with thee;

    Or, if they sleep, thy picture in my sight

    Awakes my heart to heart's and eye's delight.

047

我的眼睛和心灵结成了同盟，

它们要和衷共济，互相融通。

如果眼睛渴望看到你的芳容，

或者我的心灵受到忧伤烦扰，

我的眼睛便用你的画像举办宴会，

以色彩斑斓的画宴款待我的心灵。

有时心灵也会邀请眼睛做客，

将其藏在深处的挚爱分享给眼睛。

这样，借助你的美颜画像和我的挚爱，

我心与你紧密相连，尽管你与我想距遥远。

即使你在天涯，我心依然紧紧相牵，

剪不断的情思永远把你惦念。

  如果我的情思入睡，眼中你的画像

  也会将其唤醒，让心灵与眼睛共赏。

048

How careful was I when I took my way,

Each trifle under truest bars to thrust,

That, to my use, it might unused stay

From hands of falsehood, in sure wards of trust!

But thou, to whom my jewels trifles are,

Most worthy comfort, now my greatest grief,

Thou, best of dearest and mine only care,

Art left the prey of every vulgar thief.

Thee have I not lock'd up in any chest,

Save where thou art not, though I feel thou art,

Within the gentle closure of my breast,

From whence at pleasure thou mayst come and part;

And even thence thou wilt be stol'n, I fear,

For truth proves thievish for a prize so dear.

048

启程上路前我如此小心，

把一些用品都装箱锁紧，

万无一失谨防小偷盗窃，

确保使用时完好无损！

与你相比，我的珠宝一文不名，

你曾令我欢愉，如今却让我楚痛。

你是我的心肝，我唯一的惦念，

现在毫无防范地暴露给小偷的魔爪。

未将你锁在我心头的珠宝箱，

我觉得你应在我温情的心宇，

可不知你去了何地，只留下一座空房——

这里，你可无约无束、任意徜徉。

　　即使把你藏在我的心房也担心被偷窃，

　　因为面对如此珍贵宝物，连谦谦君子也会成梁上君子。

049

Against that time, if ever that time come,

When I shall see thee frown on my defects,

Whenas thy love hath cast his utmost sum,

Call'd to that audit by advis'd respects;

Against that time when thou shalt strangely pass

And scarcely greet me with that sun, thine eye,

When love, converted from the thing it was,

Shall reasons find of settled gravity, —

Against that time do I ensconce me here

Within the knowledge of mine own desert,

And this my hand against myself uprear,

To guard the lawful reasons on thy part.

　　　To leave poor me thou hast the strength of laws,

　　　Since, why to love, I can allege no cause.

049

我生怕有那么一天真的会到来——

你双眉紧锁，单单盯着我的缺点，

你挥霍了爱人的最后一笔钱，

经过深思熟虑要与我清算。

我生怕有那么一天，你如陌路从我身边走过，

不再用你那太阳般的眼睛向我问候，

没有了往日的情真意切，

却竭力寻找冠冕堂皇的借口。

我生怕有那么一天，于是躲藏在这里，

闭门思过，深刻反省自己的缺点，

举起我的手宣誓为你作证——

为你指控我的种种合法理由辩护。

　　你有合法的理由抛弃可怜的我。

　　而我爱你，却说不出任何理由。

050

How heavy do I journey on the way,

When what I seek — my weary travel's end,

Doth teach that ease and that repose to say,

"Thus far the miles are measur'd from thy friend!"

The beast that bears me, tired with my woe,

Plods dully on, to bear that weight in me,

As if by some instinct the wretch did know

His rider loved not speed, being made from thee:

The bloody spur cannot provoke him on

That sometimes anger thrusts into his hide;

Which heavily he answers with a groan,

More sharp to me than spurring to his side;

For that same groan doth put this in my mind;

My grief lies onward and my joy behind.

050

当我抵达这疲倦旅行的终点，

安歇的惬意和甜美的睡梦提醒我：

"你已离开朋友很远很远"，

我才意识到经历了多么忧郁的一次长途跋涉！

路上，身下的坐骑不堪我的哀愁，

驮着我沉重的忧伤蹒跚前行。

这可怜的家伙好像有某种本能，

知道主人不愿离开你而慢悠悠前行。

有时因焦急用马刺对它猛踢，

血淋淋的马刺也难催它快走，

它只是用一声沉沉呻吟来回应，

我听了后心如刀绞，比马刺刺它还要痛。

　　这呻吟在我脑海激起类似的哀叹：

　　噢，往前是忧愁，欢乐在身后！

051

Thus can my love excuse the slow offence

Of my dull bearer when from thee I speed:

From where thou art why should I haste me thence?

Till I return, of posting is no need.

O, what excuse will my poor beast then find,

When swift extremity can seem but slow?

Then should I spur, though mounted on the wind;

In wingèd speed no motion shall I know:

Then can no horse with my desire keep pace;

Therefore desire of, perfect'st love being made,

Shall neigh — no dull flesh — in his fiery race;

But love, for love, thus shall excuse my jade;

  Since from thee going he went wilful slow,

  Towards thee I'll run, and give him leave to go.

051

我的爱，这样说来我离你远行时

你原谅了我的老马慢悠悠的步履——

可离开你我又何须行色匆匆？

待我踏上回程之路时，我再策马扬鞭。

那时我岂能原谅这可怜的老马磨磨蹭蹭？

即使它快若流星我也觉得像乌龟爬行，

即使我乘风飞驰我还要用马刺策动，

即使风驰电掣我也感觉不到在前行，

没有哪匹马能赶得上我炽热的爱火。

这由至诚至爱所铸成的爱火，

完全超越麻木不仁的肉体及其匆匆步履，

那么，我的爱，为了爱，就原谅我的老马吧：

　　离开你时它故意慢慢腾腾；

　　归来时我下马向你飞奔，任马儿去磨磨蹭蹭。

052

So am I as the rich whose blessed key

Can bring him to his sweet up-lockèd treasure,

The which he will not every hour survey,

For blunting the fine point of seldom pleasure.

Therefore are feasts so solemn and so rare,

Since, seldom coming, in the long year set,

Like stones of worth they thinly placèd are,

Or captain jewels in the carcanet.

So is the time that keeps you as my chest,

Or as the wardrobe which the robe doth hide,

To make some special instant special blest,

By new unfolding his imprison'd pride.

> Blessèd are you, whose worthiness gives scope,
> Being had, to triumph, being lack'd, to hope.

052

我就像个富翁，怀揣着幸福的钥匙，

可随时开启那大门紧锁的宝库。

我不会时不时就来这里察看，

因为担心那样看到宝藏的快感会变迟钝。

节日为何显得那么庄严、稀罕？

就是因为在漫长的一年中难得一遇，

就像金项圈上的稀世珍珠宝石，

总是稀稀落落地点缀镶嵌在上面。

同样珍贵的还有那一段时光，

彼时你就像我宝盒中宝石或衣柜中的华服，

每每打开看到里面引以为傲的珍宝那一刻，

顿生一股格外幸福的暖流在心头。

　　你就是幸福的化身，无限幸运萦回在你身边；

　　有你在，欢乐无限；你不在，我把秋水望穿。

053

What is your substance, whereof are you made,

That millions of strange shadows on you tend?

Since every one hath, every one, one shade,

And you, but one, can every shadow lend.

Describe Adonis, and the counterfeit

Is poorly imitatèd after you;

On Helen's cheek all art of beauty set,

And you in Grecian tires are painted new:

Speak of the spring and foison of the year;

The one doth shadow of your beauty show,

The other as your bounty doth appear;

And you in every blessèd shape we know.

 In all external grace you have some part,

  But you like none, none you, for constant heart.

053

你究竟是由何物生成，

却有成千上万人追随你，如影随形？

人人有身影，且一人一影，

而你一人却生出身影如此之众——

若把你比作阿多尼斯①，

他的肖像只不过是对你的拙劣临摹；

若比作海伦②，尽管她脸上用尽了美容绝技，

也只不过是你身着希腊古装的画像而已；

若用一年中的芳春和金秋作比方，

前者就是你貌美的缩影，

后者就是你富贵的写真，

你是人间所有美质的化身。

　　外表优雅美丽的特质你都有，

　　但若论忠贞不渝的心，你却与众人不同。

---

① 阿多尼斯（Adonis）：希腊神话中的美少年，爱神维纳斯仰慕的情人。——译者注
② 海伦（Helen）：希腊神话中的第一美女。——译者注

054

O, how much more doth beauty beauteous seem

By that sweet ornament which truth doth give!

The rose looks fair, but fairer we it deem

For that sweet odour which doth in it live.

The canker-blooms have full as deep a dye

As the perfum'd tincture of the roses,

Hang on such thorns and play as wantonly

When summer's breath their mask'd buds discloses:

But, for their virtue only is their show,

They live unwoo'd and unrespected fade,

Die to themselves. Sweet roses do not so;

Of their sweet deaths are sweetest odours made.

　　　And so of you, beauteous and lovely youth,

　　　When that shall fade, by verse distills your truth.

054

假如用真来为美做装点，

美便更加大放异彩。

玫瑰本已很美，但人们觉得她更美，

就是因为她散发醉人的芳香。

绽放的野蔷薇色泽艳丽，

看上去与芳香四溢的玫瑰并无异样；

当夏风吹开其含苞待放的蓓蕾，

挂在枝头摇曳，妩媚妖娆，

但是其美仅仅是艳丽的外表，

绽放无人欣羡，凋谢无人惜怜，

怎能与美丽芬芳的玫瑰争妍！

玫瑰虽死亦馨扬，芳香提炼漂四方。

　　　你就是玫瑰，青春韶华芬芳娇艳，

　　　韶华逝去时，你的纯真便留在我的诗篇。

055

Not marble, nor the gilded monuments

Of princes, shall outlive this powerful rhyme;

But you shall shine more bright in these contents

Than unswept stone besmear'd with sluttish time.

When wasteful war shall statues overturn,

And broils root out the work of masonry,

Nor Mars his sword nor war's quick fire shall burn

The living record of your memory.

'Gainst death and all-oblivious enmity

Shall you pace forth; your praise shall still find room

Even in the eyes of all posterity

That wear this world out to the ending doom.

    So, till the judgment that yourself arise,

    You live in this, and dwell in lover's eyes.

055

帝王用雕像或镶金碑纪念其伟业，

但都不会像我这诗章雄文能千古流芳。

你乘着诗的翅膀高翔，更是熠熠闪光，

远胜过沾满流逝岁月陈迹的石碑、雕像。

残酷的战争会掀翻石碑，

骚乱和暴动会摧毁雕像、牌坊。

无论战神的利剑还是熊熊战火，

都不能毁掉这诗章所铭记的荣光。

你不惧死亡和诋毁，昂首阔步向前，

这诗文对你的赞颂

将在子孙后代眼中永驻，

你的美名将百世流芳，直到地老天荒。

  直到你在起身面对最后审判的时刻，

  你永远活在恋人的眼中和我这诗行！

056

Sweet love, renew thy force; be it not said

Thy edge should blunter be than appetite,

Which but today by feeding is allay'd,

Tomorrow sharpen'd in his former might:

So, love, be thou; although today thou fill

Thy hungry eyes even till they wink with fullness,

Tomorrow see again, and do not kill

The spirit of love with a perpetual dullness.

Let this sad interim like the ocean be

Which parts the shore, where two contracted new

Come daily to the banks, that, when they see

Return of love, more blest may be the view;

Else call it winter, which, being full of care

Makes summer's welcome thrice more wish'd, more rare.

056

我的爱，快让你爱的活力重生，
别让人说爱欲还比不上食欲。
食欲使今天酒足饭饱，
明日又让你饥饿如初。
我的爱，你也一样，
今日满足了爱的饥渴，直至双眼闭紧，
明日还应把盈盈秋波送给爱侣，
切勿用倦怠目光让爱的火焰窒息。
就让这阴郁的间歇如同海洋，
把两岸分开，隔海相望，
新定情的恋人天天来到海滨，
每当看到爱潮汹涌复归，欣喜无比。
　　或让这间隔成为冬季，充满忧郁，
　　这会令人对夏天更期冀、更珍惜。

057

Being your slave, what should I do but tend

Upon the hours and times of your desire?

I have no precious time at all to spend,

Nor services to do, till you require.

Nor dare I chide the world-without-end hour

Whilst I, my sovereign, watch the clock for you,

Nor think the bitterness of absence sour

When you have bid your servant once adieu;

Nor dare I question with my jealous thought

Where you may be, or your affairs suppose,

But, like a sad slave, stay and think of nought

Save, where you are how happy you make those.

    So true a fool is love that in your will

    Though you do any thing, he thinks no ill.

057

作为奴仆我唯有忠心地侍奉你，

时时刻刻都听从你的吩咐。

我的时间都平淡无奇，庸碌闲度，

也无要务缠身，唯愿俯首帖耳；

我不敢责怪这世界绵延不绝的时光，

甘愿为你——我的至尊——看守时钟，

当你吩咐我离开、不再值守时，

尽管一腔离别之苦，我也不敢多想，

不敢以嫉妒之心去打听

您去了何方，欲意何为；

像一个可怜的奴隶，随从侍奉，什么也不敢想，

只是想：你到了哪里，就让那里的人幸福无比。

　　所以，深坠爱河时还真像个傻瓜，

　　你为所欲为，他仍视你完美无瑕。

058

That god forbid that made me first your slave,

I should in thought control your times of pleasure,

Or at your hand the account of hours to crave,

Being your vassal, bound to stay your leisure!

O, let me suffer, being at your beck,

The imprison'd absence of your liberty,

And patience, tame to sufferance, bide each cheque

Without accusing you of injury.

Be where you list, your charter is so strong

That you yourself may privilege your time

To what you will; to you it doth belong

Yourself to pardon of self-doing crime.

    I am to wait, though waiting so be hell;

    Not blame your pleasure, be it ill or well.

058

当初使我成为你奴隶的神明，

禁止我萌生掌控你行乐时光的念头，

也不能有弄清你行乐时光的企图。

既然是你的奴隶，只得任你放浪。

既然听命于你，我就得默默忍受——

对你放荡不羁熟视无睹；

面对你的苛责，我必须隐忍和逆来顺受，

你深深伤害我，我却一声也不抱怨，

无论你高兴去哪儿，你至高无上的特权

让你任意支配你的时间和行藏，

无所顾忌地为所欲为，

并把你的一切罪责全赦免。

　　　我只好等待，哪怕像在人间地狱熬煎，

　　　绝不指责你作乐寻欢，任凭是恶还是善。

059

If there be nothing new, but that which is

Hath been before, how are our brains beguil'd,

Which, labouring for invention, bear amiss

The second burden of a former child!

O, that record could with a backward look,

Even of five hundred courses of the sun,

Show me your image in some antique book,

Since mind at first in character was done!

That I might see what the old world could say

To this compos'd wonder of your frame;

Whether we are mend'd, or whe'er better they,

Or whether revolution be the same.

    O, sure I am, the wits of former days

    To subjects worse have given admiring praise.

059

如果世间无新生事物而一成不变，
我们还枉费心机地发明创造，
等于误让曾有的孩子又生一遍，
那对我们的大脑是多大的糜耗！
但愿历史能让我们回溯，
回溯到太阳五百个行程之前，
斯时人的所思所想最初被文字记载，
从那时的一本古书上看到你曾经的形象！
如此，我就可以看到古人
如何评价你的形质——这个人间奇迹！
看看我们的赞美好，还是古人的评价高，
看看世间是有革新除弊，还是一成不变。
　　但有一点我敢肯定，古代的文人墨客
　　赞颂过的所有人物，全都远比你逊色。

060

Like as the waves make towards the pebbl'd shore,

So do our minutes hasten to their end;

Each changing place with that which goes before,

In sequent toil all forwards do contend.

Nativity, once in the main of light,

Crawls to maturity, wherewith being crown'd,

Crookèd elipses 'gainst his glory fight,

And Time that gave doth now his gift confound.

Time doth transfix the flourish set on youth

And delves the parallels in beauty's brow,

Feeds on the rarities of nature's truth,

And nothing stands but for his scythe to mow.

　　　And yet to times in hope my verse shall stand,

　　　Praising thy worth, despite his cruel hand.

060

像汹涌的海浪拍击布满砂石的海岸，
人生的时光匆匆涌向终点，
后浪推前浪，无限绵延，
接续前行，奋力争先。
一旦生命诞生沐浴阳光雨露，
便不断成熟，达到光辉顶点；
而邪恶的日食却要阴翳生命之光，
时间暴君又将其送出的礼物捣烂，
把青春的美饰刺得粉碎，
在美丽的额头挖掘道道沟壑，
最终蚕食掉这美丽的稀世珍宝，
万物难逃时间暴君的风剑霜刀！
　　但是，我这诗章能逃他的毒手，
　　让你的美名永驻，万古流芳。

061

Is it thy will thy image should keep open

My heavy eyelids to the weary night?

Dost thou desire my slumbers should be broken,

While shadows, like to thee, do mock my sight?

Is it thy spirit that thou send'st from thee

So far from home into my deeds to pry,

To find out shames and idle hours in me,

The scope and tenor of thy jealousy?

O, no! thy love, though much, is not so great:

It is my love that keeps mine eye awake;

Mine own true love that doth my rest defeat,

To play the watchman ever for thy sake:

     For thee watch I whilst thou dost wake elsewhere,

     From me far off, with others all-too-near.

061

你是否非要用你的倩影让我不眠，

在漫漫遥夜中静静地睁着双眼？

难道你真的要用你的倩影，

把我从美梦中惊醒，然后嘲笑我的眼睛？

你是否派你的芳魂，

远离魂舍来刺探我的行藏，

找寻我的不轨和放浪，

查明你猜忌的原委——

看看你对我的妒爱有多重，嫉情有多深？

噢，不，你对我虽有爱但情不深；

是我对你的爱让我难以合眼，

是我对你的情使我难以入眠。

是为了你我才扮演这守夜人。

　　我在夜里守望着你，而你也在熬夜，

　　只是背着我在别处与别人卿卿我我。

062

Sin of self-love possesseth all mine eye,

And all my soul and all my every part;

And for this sin there is no remedy,

It is so grounded inward in my heart.

Methinks no face so gracious is as mine,

No shape so true, no truth of such account;

And for myself mine own worth do define,

As I all other in all worths surmount.

But when my glass shows me myself indeed,

Beated and chopp'd with tann'd antiquity,

Mine own self-love quite contrary I read;

Self so self-loving were iniquity.

　　'Tis thee — myself — that for myself I praise,

　　Painting my age with beauty of thy days.

062

自恋不仅霸占了我的双眼，

还充斥于我的身躯和灵魂。

我的自恋病尚无良方可救，

因为它植根于我内心深处。

我以为我的美貌旷世无双，

我的形体和真诚独占鳌头。

我自身的价值无人能敌，

方方面面都卓尔超群。

但是当我在镜子里看到真实的自己：

满脸风刀刻痕尽显岁月沧桑。

我的自恋同真实的自己大相径庭，

自我迷恋真的无异于罪戾劣行。

    原来，我对自己的赞颂是在赞颂你，

    是用你的青春粉饰我的苍桑与衰靡。

063

Against my love shall be, as I am now,

With Time's injurious hand crush'd and o'er-worn;

When hours have drain'd his blood and fill'd his brow

With lines and wrinkles; when his youthful morn

Hath travell'd on to age's steepy night,

And all those beauties whereof now he's king

Are vanishing or vanish'd out of sight,

Stealing away the treasure of his spring;

For such a time do I now fortify

Against confounding age's cruel knife,

That he shall never cut from memory

My sweet love's beauty, though my lover's life:

　　His beauty shall in these black lines be seen,

　　And they shall live, and he in them still green.

063

吾爱也将会和我现在一样，

被时间暴君的毒手销蚀和摧残，

那时，时间暴君会把他的鲜血吸干，

并在他额头上把皱纹刻满；

他朝阳般的青春历经跋涉步入幽谷般的暮年；

虽然他现在一切美质卓越超群，

但终将会不断销蚀，直到消泯——

他青春的瑰宝也将被时间盗去；

为预防这一天的到来，我筑牢深壑高垒，

以阻挡无情岁月的残暴芒刀

斩断对吾爱之美的永久怀念，

尽管它斩断了吾爱的生命。

　　吾爱之美将永驻这些字里行间，

　　这诗将永存，吾爱也随之永生。

064

When I have seen by Time's fell hand defac'd

The rich proud cost of outworn buried age;

When sometime lofty towers I see down-raz'd

And brass eternal slave to mortal rage;

When I have seen the hungry ocean gain

Advantage on the kingdom of the shore,

And the firm soil win of the watery main,

Increasing store with loss and loss with store;

When I have seen such interchange of state,

Or state itself confounded to decay;

Ruin hath taught me thus to ruminate —

That Time will come and take my love away.

    This thought is as a death, which cannot choose

    But weep to have that which it fears to lose.

064

当我看到时间暴君凶恶的黑手
毁掉历代遗留的浮华富丽；
当我看到巍峨高楼崩塌成为瓦砾，
石雕铜像在暴乱中被遗弃；
当我看到饥饿的大海之口张开，
把海岸的城邦吞噬，
不屈的土地又复填大片海域，
得而复失，失而复回，周而复始。
当我看到万物更迭交替，循环往复，
万物也自我毁灭消亡，
此刻，历史遗迹告诉我应这样想：
时间老人最终会来把吾爱带到天堂。
　　此念令人绝望，但乃人生宿命，
　　我只有为担心失去吾爱而哀伤。

065

Since brass, nor stone, nor earth, nor boundless sea,

But sad mortality o'er-sways their power,

How with this rage shall beauty hold a plea,

Whose action is no stronger than a flower?

O, how shall summer's honey breath hold out

Against the wreckful siege of battering days,

When rocks impregnable are not so stout,

Nor gates of steel so strong, but Time decays?

O fearful meditation! where, alack,

Shall Time's best jewel from Time's chest lie hid?

Or what strong hand can hold his swift foot back?

Or who his spoil of beauty can forbid?

    O, none, unless this miracle have might,

    That in black ink my love may still shine bright.

065

铜雕、石碑、大地和苍茫海洋，

都将逃不过灭亡的下场。

那么，美人柔弱如芬芳，

何以敌过死神的狂妄？

夏日香花碧草郁弥，

何以敌得过未来寒日酷宵？

石碑虽坚，钢门虽牢，

何以敌得过时间的蚀销？

啊！愈想愈胆寒！

来自时间宝盒①的时间珍宝②可到哪里躲藏？

可有巨手能拦住这时间的匆匆步履？

或者有谁能阻止它毁玉消香？

　　　没有，只有我这神奇的笔有此力量，

　　　它可让吾爱在黑色墨迹中永放光芒！

───────────────

① 时间宝盒：等同于西方文化中的造物主。——译者注

② 来自时间宝盒的时间珍宝：也即造物主所造万物，包括上面列举的铜雕、石碑、大地、海洋、钢门、鲜花，乃至美人等。——译者注

066

Tired with all these, for restful death I cry:

As, to behold desert a beggar born,

And needy nothing trimm'd in jollity,

And purest faith unhappily forsworn,

And gilded honour shamefully misplac'd,

And maiden virtue rudely strumpeted,

And right perfection wrongfully disgrac'd,

And strength by limping sway disablèd,

And art made tongue-tied by authority,

And folly doctor-like controlling skill,

And simple truth miscall'd simplicity,

And captive good attending captain ill:

     Tir'd with all these, from these would I be gone,

     Save that, to die, I leave my love alone.

066

宁愿赴黄泉，只缘厌恶世不平——

譬如我目睹的英杰俊才成乞丐，

譬如平庸之辈穿金戴银神采扬，

譬如忠贞不渝者遭抛弃，

譬如授勋封爵张冠戴在李头上，

譬如纯真少女被蹂躏，

譬如光明正义遭诬陷，

譬如好汉却遭跛脚欺，

譬如艺术自由被压制，

譬如假博学摇身成"才子"，

譬如歪曲纯真为愚昧，

譬如善民却为恶霸当奴隶。

　　厌倦了这一切，真想以死来消万古愁，

　　只是担心身后留下吾爱独自愁。

067

Ah, wherefore with infection should he live,

And with his presence grace impiety,

That sin by him advantage should achieve

And lace itself with his society?

Why should false painting imitate his cheek

And steal dead seeing of his living hue?

Why should poor beauty indirectly seek

Roses of shadow, since his rose is true?

Why should he live, now Nature bankrupt is,

Beggar'd of blood to blush through lively veins?

For she hath no exchequer now but his,

And, proud of many, lives upon his gains.

    O, him she stores, to show what wealth she had

    In days long since, before these last so bad.

067

噢，他为什么生活在这浊世，

还用他的美丽优雅美化虚伪，

让罪孽凭借他乘机获益——

通过与他交际来美化自己？

为什么让赝品画临摹他的美貌，

把他飞扬的神采画得神情呆滞？

这可怜的美人既然他是笃真的玫瑰，

为什么还舍近求远去寻求玫瑰的花影？

现在造物主都已倾家荡产，没有了新鲜血液

输入他的的血管，为什么他还苟且于世？

因为她①除了他的美再无美的财富，

她之所以仍夸口说腰缠万贯②，只缘能从他身上获取③。

　　她为证明在此浊世很久以前自己曾拥有

　　美之财富，才把他留在世间未予召回。

---

① 她：指大自然，即西方文化里的造物主。——译者注

② 这里腰缠万贯，指具有很多美的财富。——译者注

③ 以此来夸张指称"他"之美。——译者注

068

Thus is his cheek the map of days outworn,

When beauty liv'd and died as flowers do now,

Before the bastard signs of fair were born,

Or durst inhabit on a living brow;

Before the golden tresses of the dead,

The right of sepulchres, were shorn away,

To live a second life on second head;

Ere beauty's dead fleece made another gay:

In him those holy antique hours are seen,

Without all ornament, itself and true,

Making no summer of another's green,

Robbing no old to dress his beauty new;

    And him as for a map doth Nature store,

    To show false Art what beauty was of yore.

068

他的脸庞是往昔岁月的图景，

那时花开花谢无异于今朝的情形，

那时虚饰之美尚未诞生——

尚不敢对活人的脸进行粉饰。

那时死者的金色秀发可安藏于墓里，

不会横遭快剪剪除的悲惨命运①

以在他人头上再现风姿

借其让美又获重生。

所有这些昔世圣洁的时光历景，

都在他身上闪现，且无丝毫虚饰，

无需用他人的碧草香花营造自己的芬芳夏日，

无需借古装旧服的雅丽来装扮自己的新美。

　　造物主将他作为一幅美图来收藏，

　　让伪饰者见识往昔之美的真模样。

---

① 莎士比亚时代的假发制造商通过买死者的头发来制作假发。——译者注

069

Those parts of thee that the world's eye doth view

Want nothing that the thought of hearts can mend;

All tongues, the voice of souls, give thee that due,

Uttering bare truth, even so as foes commend.

Thy outward thus with outward praise is crown'd;

But those same tongues that give thee so thine own

In other accents do this praise confound

By seeing farther than the eye hath shown.

They look into the beauty of thy mind,

And that, in guess, they measure by thy deeds;

Then, churls, their thoughts, although their eyes were kind,

To thy fair flower add the rank smell of weeds:

But why thy odour matcheth not thy show,

The solve is this, that thou dost common grow.

069

你的貌美质丽点亮了世人的眼睛，

任何想象力都无法把你的美色增。

无数张嘴一起发出赞美你的心声，

这凿凿事实就连你的仇人也肯定。

众人只是对你的美貌肤浅地赞叹，

而正是那些口口声声赞美你的人

却用不同的声音又将其赞美诋毁，

他们能洞悉远超视觉看到的东西，

可以透过外表洞察你善美的心灵；

且常以臆测揣度来评价你行止。

他们虽然双眼宽宏，心眼却狭纤无比，

不惜将你美丽花朵洒上杂草的恶臭。

　　　为什么你的花香比不上你的花美？

　　　只缘你生长在了庸凡的土壤里。

070

That thou art blam'd shall not be thy defect,

For slander's mark was ever yet the fair;

The ornament of beauty is suspect,

A crow that flies in heaven's sweetest air.

So thou be good, slander doth but approve

Thy worth the greater, being woo'd of time;

For canker vice the sweetest buds doth love,

And thou present'st a pure unstained prime.

Thou hast pass'd by the ambush of young days,

Either not assail'd or victor being charg'd;

Yet this thy praise cannot be so thy praise,

To tie up envy evermore enlarg'd:

    If some suspect of ill mask'd not thy show,

    Then thou alone kingdoms of hearts shouldst owe.

070

你受谩骂指责并非是你的错，

美人向来是流言蜚语的箭靶。

猜忌本身恰恰是对美的装点，

就像一只乌鸦飞到碧蓝长空。

你德美心善，流言会不攻自破，

更证明你至善至美，时代楷模，

因为害虫最爱藏匿在娇美的花蕾。

你处于风华正茂时纯洁无瑕，

你能度过青春路上的埋伏，

不是未受伏击，就是已将其攻克。

可是，对你这样的赞美不足以

束缚漫天横飞的嫉妒的翅膀。

　　假如恶意猜忌掩盖不住你的荣光，

　　那么你就会独占无数的心灵城邦。

071

No longer mourn for me when I am dead

Than you shall hear the surly sullen bell

Give warning to the world that I am fled

From this vile world, with vilest worms to dwell.

Nay, if you read this line, remember not

The hand that writ it; for I love you so

That I in your sweet thoughts would be forgot

If thinking on me then should make you woe.

O, if, I say, you look upon this verse

When I perhaps compounded am with clay,

Do not so much as my poor name rehearse;

But let your love even with my life decay,

> Lest the wise world should look into your moan
>
> And mock you with me after I am gone.

071

当我离开人世时切勿为我哀悼，

那时你会听到阴沉的丧钟敲响，

向世人宣告我已从这浊世逃离，

去往另一个世界陪伴了了蝇蛆。

若你读到这诗，别惦记出自谁人之手，

因为我是如此的爱你，

宁愿你在你甜美的记忆中把我遗忘，

以免在你美好思绪里想起我而悲伤

噢，我觉得当你看到此诗之际，

我也许早已融入泥土；

切勿再总提我这卑微的名字，

姑且让你对我的爱与我的生命一同化作青烟飞逝，

　　　　以免博学才俊们看透你内心的哀伤，

　　　　在我死后拿我当笑柄来把你嘲讽。

072

O, lest the world should task you to recite

What merit liv'd in me, that you should love

After my death, dear love, forget me quite,

For you in me can nothing worthy prove;

Unless you would devise some virtuous lie,

To do more for me than mine own desert,

And hang more praise upon deceasèd I

Than niggard truth would willingly impart:

O, lest your true love may seem false in this,

That you for love speak well of me untrue,

My name be buried where my body is,

And live no more to shame nor me nor you.

  For I am sham'd by that which I bring forth,

  And so should you, to love things nothing worth.

072

我的至爱，我死后把我彻底忘记，
因为你无法向人证明我超凡卓群，
以免让世人刨根问底，向你追问
我到底好在哪里，值得你如此钟爱。
你只好编织一些善意的不实之词，
对我的功名言过其实地夸赞，
给已经谢世的我太多荣耀——
远远超过这个吝啬现实世界的意愿。
这会使人觉得你对我的真情是假意，
你是为了爱才罔顾事实把我说得天花乱坠。
让我的名字随我的身体一起埋葬，
别让其留给后世令你我都受中伤。
　　我早就因自己已面世的拙作而羞愧，
　　你也将会因爱了这不值所爱而懊悔。

073

That time of year thou mayst in me behold

When yellow leaves, or none, or few, do hang

Upon those boughs which shake against the cold,

Bare ruin'd choirs, where late the sweet birds sang.

In me thou seest the twilight of such day

As after sunset fadeth in the west,

Which by and by black night doth take away,

Death's second self, that seals up all in rest.

In me thou seest the glowing of such fire

That on the ashes of his youth doth lie,

As the death-bed whereon it must expire

Consumed with that which it was nourish'd by.

    This thou perceivest, which makes thy love more strong,

    To love that well which thou must leave ere long.

073

你在我身上会看到这样的时刻，

那时或黄叶满树，或残叶零丁，

挂在树枝上在寒风中瑟瑟颤抖，

不久前百鸟鸣啭的歌坛①变得荒凉颓废。

当你在我身上看到了秋日的黄昏，

宛如夕阳消失于西边的地平线，

被黑沉沉的夜幕渐渐地吞噬，

像死神的替身把安息的万物遮盖。

在我身上你能看到这样的火焰——

在青春的灰烬上依然辉光熠熠

临终时在病榻上渐渐熄灭，

与供给它的燃料一起耗尽。

　　　你觉察到这一切，就会爱得愈加历久弥坚，

　　　对不久即将离你而去的人更加挚爱和珍重。

---

① 歌坛：喻指上文所提到的树，因为此前鸟儿在上面鸣啭歌唱。——译者注

074

But be contented: when that fell arrest

Without all bail shall carry me away,

My life hath in this line some interest,

Which for memorial still with thee shall stay.

When thou reviewest this, thou dost review

The very part was consecrate to thee.

The earth can have but earth, which is his due;

My spirit is thine, the better part of me:

So then thou hast but lost the dregs of life,

The prey of worms, my body being dead;

The coward conquest of a wretch's knife,

Too base of thee to be rememberèd.

  The worth of that is that which it contains,

  And that is this, and this with thee remains.

074

当地狱的差役不由分说把我带走①，

你切勿太过悲痛，

因为这诗行与我的来世相影随行，

成为永久的纪念与你相伴终生。

每当你重读这些诗行，

都能看到我专门献给你的辞章。

犹如土属于大地乃天经地义，

我诗章的精髓——我的灵魂——属于你。

因此，我的肉体一旦逝去，

你失去的不过是生命中的残渣——

蛆虫的美食和被恶棍之刀征服的懦夫——

太卑微而不值得你铭记。

　　我身躯的价值就是其内在的灵魂——

　　这不朽之诗——将会陪伴你终身！

---

① 这句话的意指死亡。——译者注

075

So are you to my thoughts as food to life,

Or as sweet-season'd showers are to the ground;

And for the peace of you I hold such strife

As 'twixt a miser and his wealth is found.

Now proud as an enjoyer and anon

Doubting the filching age will steal his treasure;

Now counting best to be with you alone,

Then better'd that the world may see my pleasure;

Sometime all full with feasting on your sight

And by and by clean starvèd for a look;

Possessing or pursuing no delight,

Save what is had or must from you be took.

> Thus do I pine and surfeit day by day,
>
> Or gluttoning on all, or all away.

075

你之于我思想如食物之于生命，

恰似春日甘霖沐浴大地。

在尽享爱你的宁静中却备感心绪不宁，

犹如守财奴总担心财宝被盗的心情：

时而得意洋洋，活像天之骄子，

时而担心这偷盗泛滥的年代财宝被盗光；

时而觉得最宝贵的时光莫过于与你独处，

时而又想向世人炫耀自己得意于情场；

时而觉得凝视你才能填饱饥饿的双眼，

时而觉得淡淡一瞥漫送秋波心里则更美更甜。

我唯独想获得与你独处的快乐，

除此以外，对所有快乐我都不奢求。

　　我就是这样日复一日地饱餐与饥饿交迭不止；

　　要么饕餮盛餐，要么食不果腹。

076

Why is my verse so barren of new pride,

So far from variation or quick change?

Why, with the time, do I not glance aside

To new-found methods and to compounds strange?

Why write I still all one, ever the same,

And keep invention in a noted weed,

That every word doth almost tell my name,

Showing their birth and where they did proceed?

O, know, sweet love, I always write of you,

And you and love are still my argument;

So all my best is dressing old words new,

Spending again what is already spent.

    For as the sun is daily new and old,

    So is my love still telling what is told.

076

为什么我的诗缺乏新风采，

呆板单调，缺少神来之笔？

为什么我不跟上时代步履，

用时尚的方法和绮词丽句？

为什么我的作品主题雷同，

表现手法也总是千篇一律，

几乎每个词都标着我的名字，

显示源于何处，用意何为？

噢，可你知道，我的至爱，

我只写你和爱这个永恒的主题，

尽我所能让旧词添新义，

穷我所思让旧曲添新声。

　　正如日出日落轮回旧日换新阳，

　　我对你的爱日夜倾诉也不觉是滥调陈腔。

077

Thy glass will show thee how thy beauties wear,

Thy dial how thy precious minutes waste;

The vacant leaves thy mind's imprint will bear,

And of this book this learning mayst thou taste.

The wrinkles which thy glass will truly show

Of mouthèd graves will give thee memory;

Thou by thy dial's shady stealth mayst know

Time's thievish progress to eternity.

Look, what thy memory can not contain

Commit to these waste blanks, and thou shalt find

Those children nurs'd, deliver'd from thy brain,

To take a new acquaintance of thy mind.

 These offices, so oft as thou wilt look,

 Shall profit thee and much enrich thy book.

077

镜子会告诉你你的美貌如何消靡，

日晷会告诉你你的青春如何流逝。

这些空白页①会留下你心灵的印迹，

你或许从中体味此书给你的教益。

镜子可如实地照出你的丝丝皱纹，

使你联想到张着大口的荒坟。

日晷渐渐移动的影子会让你懂得，

时间老人的脚步正悄悄迈向永恒。

瞧！凡是你脑海包容不了的东西，

都可交付给这些空白页来承负，

你会发现你脑海里孕育出的儿女，

将再次与你的心灵相识、相融。

　　　　你若经常照镜子、观日晷、记录心历路程②，

　　　　你将受益良多，会让你的空白页不断丰盈。

---

① 许多莎士比亚研究专家认为，此诗连同一个作为礼物的笔记本一道送给朋友。"这些空
　白页"即指该笔记本。——译者注

② 此句英语原文为 These offices, so oft as thou wilt look. 其中 These offices 指上文提到的照镜
　子、观日晷、（在空白页上）记心得等。——译者注

078

So oft have I invok'd thee for my Muse

And found such fair assistance in my verse

As every alien pen hath got my use,

And under thee their poesy disperse.

Thine eyes that taught the dumb on high to sing

And heavy ignorance aloft to fly,

Have added feathers to the learnèd's wing

And given grace a double majesty.

Yet be most proud of that which I compile,

Whose influence is thine and born of thee:

In others' works thou dost but mend the style,

And arts with thy sweet graces graced be;

　　But thou art all my art and dost advance

　　As high as learning my rude ignorance.

078

我经常将你当诗神来乞求灵感，

我的诗章到处闪现着你的灵光，

于是许多陌生诗人纷纷效仿，

其诗作沐浴着你的灵光四海传扬。

你的双眼曾教会哑巴高声放歌，

还教会无知愚昧插翅高翔，

你让饱学之士的翅膀翎满羽丰，

还赋予鸿儒雅士以凌厉威严。

你完全可为我写的诗作而自豪，

因为你的诗魂是它们的滥觞。

而对别的诗人你只须润色其风格，

使他们的诗篇辞藻华丽、神采飞扬。

　　　我的诗才都源于你的诗魂，

　　　是你让我从粗陋无知变得学识博广。

079

Whilst I alone did call upon thy aid,

My verse alone had all thy gentle grace,

But now my gracious numbers are decay'd

And my sick Muse doth give another place.

I grant, sweet love, thy lovely argument

Deserves the travail of a worthier pen,

Yet what of thee thy poet doth invent

He robs thee of and pays it thee again.

He lends thee virtue and he stole that word

From thy behavior; beauty doth he give

And found it in thy cheek; he can afford

No praise to thee but what in thee doth live.

    Then thank him not for that which he doth say,

    Since what he owes thee thou thyself dost pay.

079

当初我独自乞求你赐予我灵感，

我的诗浸透着你柔美典雅的风范。

但是如今我笔下似乎思竭词穷，

我那荼靡的诗神也应当让位。

亲爱的，我须承认，你这美妙的主题，

须由才华横溢的诗人来笔工，

而他搜肠刮肚寻词觅句对你的赞颂，

只不过是窃你之美，还你之俊。

他称赞你道德高尚，那源于你品正行端，

他称颂你貌美绝伦，那是你脸天生质艳，

他倾其全力对你的所有称赞，

无一不是你自身之美的再现。

　　　既然他只是把欠你的予以偿还，

　　　你就无须感谢他对你的讴歌与称赞。

080

O, how I faint when I of you do write,

Knowing a better spirit doth use your name,

And in the praise thereof spends all his might

To make me tongue-tied, speaking of your fame!

But since your worth — wide as the ocean is —

The humble as the proudest sail doth bear,

My saucy bark inferior far to his,

On your broad main doth wilfully appear.

Your shallowest help will hold me up afloat,

Whilst he upon your soundless deep doth ride;

Or being wreck'd, I am a worthless boat,

He of tall building and of goodly pride.

    Then if he thrive and I be cast away,

    The worst was this; my love was my decay.

080

噢，我在写诗赞美你时心中无比惆怅，

因为得知有高手在把你的美名颂扬。

他为赞颂你堪称不遗余力，

以便让我闭口不再对你赞颂。

而你的宏德浩瀚如海，

能荡一叶扁舟，也能载巨轮宏舸。

尽管我这粗陋的小船与其巨轮云泥之别，

却仍愿到你的茫茫沧海起航扬帆

尽管他疾驰在你的深海滔滔，

我可以浮游在你的浅水漪涟。

即使遇险，我是一条一文不名的小船，

而他是桅高舸巨，自信一定能脱险。

　　　因此，如果他如日中天而我被你遗弃，

　　　那最糟也不过是我对你的爱随我一同消逝。

081

Or I shall live your epitaph to make,

Or you survive when I in earth am rotten;

From hence your memory death cannot take,

Although in me each part will be forgotten.

Your name from hence immortal life shall have,

Though I, once gone, to all the world must die;

The earth can yield me but a common grave,

When you entombed in men's eyes shall lie.

Your monument shall be my gentle verse,

Which eyes not yet created shall o'er-read,

And tongues to be, your being shall rehearse

When all the breathers of this world are dead.

    You still shall live — such virtue hath my pen —

    Where breath most breathes, even in the mouths of men.

081

不管是我活着为你写墓志铭，

还是你活着见证我埋入坟茔，

死神都不能抹去你的美名，

而我却被人们遗忘得干干净净。

你的美名从此万古流芳，

而我一旦离世却留不下任何踪迹。

大地只给我一方再普通不过的墓穴，

而你却永驻于世人的一双双眼睛。

你的墓碑就是我这温情的诗篇，

纵使现在世界上的生灵消逝的无踪无影，

未来世人的眼睛会百读不厌，

也将口口相传把你的美名称赞。

　　你将永远活在人们心中——吾笔有此神功，

　　只要人们呼吸不止，他们将交口称颂你的英名。

082

I grant thou wert not married to my Muse,

And therefore mayst without attaint o'erlook

The dedicated words which writers use

Of their fair subject, blessing every book.

Thou art as fair in knowledge as in hue,

Finding thy worth a limit past my praise,

And therefore art enforc'd to seek anew

Some fresher stamp of the time-bettering days.

And do so, love; yet when they have devis'd

What strain'd touches rhetoric can lend,

Thou truly fair wert truly sympathiz'd

In true plain words, by thy true-telling friend;

    And their gross painting might be better us'd

    Where cheeks need blood; in thee it is abus'd.

082

我承认你从未曾与我的诗神有过姻缘，

因此你可以问心无愧地去披阅

作家们以你为美丽主题的诗篇，

你为他们所有的诗作都赋予灵感。

你的学识卓越，你的美貌超凡，

我才疏学浅，难以写尽你的美质美德

因而你需要另觅高明——

让那些盛世才俊中的新秀把你赞颂。

我的爱，当他们穷尽其修辞手段——

华丽的辞藻带有几分牵强的造作时，

你最终会发现你的美质美德

都在你吐露真言的朋友朴实的诗篇。

　　浓妆，他们适合化在面黄灰肤者的脸皮，

　　而涂在你冰肌玉颜上却枉费了一片心机。

083

I never saw that you did painting need,

And therefore to your fair no painting set;

I found, or thought I found, you did exceed

The barren tender of a poet's debt;

And therefore have I slept in your report

That you yourself, being extant, well might show

How far a modern quill doth come too short,

Speaking of worth, what worth in you doth grow.

This silence for my sin you did impute,

Which shall be most my glory, being dumb;

For I impair not beauty being mute,

When others would give life and bring a tomb.

There lives more life in one of your fair eyes

Than both your poets can in praise devise.

083

我从不认为你需要画脸描眉，

所以从不往你脸上涂脂抹粉。

我发现或自认为发现你的美

远胜过诗人为报恩写的诗文。

我索性高枕入眠不再费笔墨，

让你自我展现你到底有多美多艳，

以证明那鹅毛笔①要把你的美质充分表现，

显得多么苍白无力。

你把我的沉默归于我的过错，

而这种装聋作哑恰恰是我高明之举，

因为我沉默对你的美毫发无损，

别人本想为你增添生气却枉费了心机。

　　你美丽的双眼透出的生命灵光，

　　远胜过诗人穷尽献媚辞藻的颂扬。

---

① 莎士比亚时代用鹅翎作为书写工具，这里代指诗人的修辞手法。——译者注

084

Who is it that says most, which can say more

Than this rich praise — that you alone are you?

In whose confine immurèd is the store

Which should example where your equal grew?

Lean penury within that pen doth dwell

That to his subject lends not some small glory;

But he that writes of you, if he can tell

That you are you, so dignifies his story,

Let him but copy what in you is writ,

Not making worse what nature made so clear,

And such a counterpart shall fame his wit,

Making his style admired every where.

    You to your beauteous blessings add a curse,

    Being fond on praise, which makes your praises worse.

084

有谁能道出可超越 "唯有你才是你"

这样富有深刻意蕴的绝伦妙语？

有谁的幽闭的内心能纳藏这样的美质，

可堪作像你一样的楷模？

脑海中词汇贫乏的诗人，

很难有恢弘巨制来把诗情抒发。

但他在写你时若能道出

"唯有你才是你"，那才会诗情荡漾。

要让他依样临摹你的原模原样，

切勿让他糟蹋了这造物主的绝世珍品。

这样的临摹作品会让他享誉诗坛，

他的诗风也将会受到世间的歆羡。

　　你应该对这种赞美予以痛斥，

　　沉湎于别人的赞美，赞美会变得一文不值。

085

My tongue-tied Muse in manners holds her still,

While comments of your praise, richly compil'd,

Reserve their character with golden quill

And precious phrase by all the Muses fil'd.

I think good thoughts whilst other write good words,

And like unletter'd clerk still cry "Amen"

To every hymn that able spirit affords

In polish'd form of well-refined pen.

Hearing you prais'd, I say "'Tis so,'tis true,"

And to the most of praise add something more;

But that is in my thought, whose love to you,

Though words come hindmost, holds his rank before.

　　Then others for the breath of words respect,

　　Me for my dumb thoughts, speaking in effect.

085

我缄口的诗神优雅地保持沉默，

而别的诗人却对你大唱赞歌，

用他们华丽的辞藻把你颂扬，

殊不知那些隽词是所有诗神合力雕琢。

他们用绮词粉饰，而我是从心底里祝福，

就像教堂里没有学问的牧师对其他诗人

所唱诵的每一首精心雕琢的华丽赞歌，

都要在其曲终时高喊一声"阿门"。

只要听到对你的赞美，我都要给予首肯，

且对绝美的颂词还要作润色粉饰，

这是我的一片真心，对你的挚爱，

话虽然说在最后，情却在别人的前头。

　　　因此别人出口成章对你敬颂，

　　　而我给予你此处无声胜有声的一片深情。

086

Was it the proud full sail of his great verse,

Bound for the prize of all-too-precious you,

That did my ripe thoughts in my brain inhearse,

Making their tomb the womb wherein they grew?

Was it his spirit, by spirits taught to write

Above a mortal pitch, that struck me dead?

No, neither he, nor his compeers by night

Giving him aid, my verse astonished.

He, nor that affable familiar ghost

Which nightly gulls him with intelligence

As victors of my silence cannot boast;

I was not sick of any fear from thence.

But when your countenance fill'd up his line,

Then lack'd I matter; that enfeebl'd mine.

086

难道是他鸿篇巨制的诗卷

载满宏舸前往接受你珍贵的恩赏，

令我酝酿中的诗情装入棺椁，

还未出世就将其孕育之地变成了坟冢？

难道是他的灵魂受精灵的驱使，

写出这惊世奇文，令我无地自容？

不，不是他，也不是寂夜的精灵

助他一臂之力，才令我的诗黯然失色。

他和他那位出手相助的友善精灵，

都不会让他一夜间就诗情万种，

从而夸耀让我缄口、俯首称臣；

我从此反倒无所畏惧，镇定自若！

　　　　只有在你对他的诗作赞许连连时，

　　　　我才会诗情全无，诗兴一落千尺。

087

Farewell! Thou art too dear for my possessing,

And like enough thou know'st thy estimate.

The charter of thy worth gives thee releasing;

My bonds in thee are all determinate.

For how do I hold thee but by thy granting?

And for that riches where is my deserving?

The cause of this fair gift in me is wanting,

And so my patent back again is swerving.

Thyself thou gav'st, thy own worth then not knowing,

Or me, to whom thou gav'st it, else mistaking;

So thy great gift, upon misprision growing,

Comes home again, on better judgment making.

 Thus have I had thee, as a dream doth flatter,

 In sleep a king, but waking, no such matter.

087

再见！你太高贵我难以攀附，

而你对自己身份也毫不隐晦。

你位高言重可以不受约束，

我俩之间的誓约可告终解除。

我怎能单凭你口头允诺而拥有你？

如此贵重的财宝岂配我拥有？

我想不出接受这份厚礼的理由，

所以我应把你给我的特许还回。

因为你授给我时不是尚未认请自己的高贵，

就是因疏忽选错了受惠人。

你这如此贵重的礼物因错授对象

而应物归原主，之后再斟酌授予何人。

　　我曾拥有你如幻梦一场，备感无尚骄荣，

　　梦里是君王，醒来发现是黄粱。

088

When thou shalt be dispos'd to set me light,

And place my merit in the eye of scorn,

Upon thy side against myself I'll fight,

And prove thee virtuous, though thou art forsworn.

With mine own weakness being best acquainted,

Upon thy part I can set down a story

Of faults conceal'd, wherein I am attainted,

That thou, in losing me, shalt win much glory.

And I by this will be a gainer too;

For bending all my loving thoughts on thee,

The injuries that to myself I do,

Doing thee vantage, double-vantage me.

    Such is my love, to thee I so belong,

    That for thy right myself will bear all wrong.

088

当你心底里视我轻如鸿羽，
我的优点也被你嗤之以鼻，
斯时我将会随你嫌憎自己，
你虽食言，却与高尚思齐。
我对自身的缺点深知无疑，
为了你我撒谎也在所不惜：
自称内心的狡诈登峰造极。
你虽失去我，却赢得荣誉，
而我也由此得到不菲获益；
我把所有的情思都给了你，
宁愿给自己惹来满身毁誉，
予你玫瑰，我留余香漫弥。
　　这就是吾爱：我的一切都属于你，
　　　只要为了你，我忍辱毁誉也不蒽！

089

Say that thou didst forsake me for some fault,

And I will comment upon that offence;

Speak of my lameness, and I straight will halt,

Against thy reasons making no defence.

Thou canst not, love, disgrace me half so ill,

To set a form upon desired change,

As I'll myself disgrace: knowing thy will,

I will acquaintance strangle and look strange,

Be absent from thy walks; and in my tongue

Thy sweet belov'd name no more shall dwell,

Lest I, too much profane, should do it wrong

And haply of our old acquaintance tell.

> For thee against myself I'll vow debate,
>
> For I must ne'er love him whom thou dost hate.

089

且说你负心于我是因我之过，
我愿意为你对我的指责开脱。
你说我腿瘸，我便立刻脚跛，
对你的指责我不加任何反驳。
我的爱，你为达心愿而矫作，
但无须对我的名声如此毁祸，
你欲辱我名，我便毁誉自我。
我猜透你的恶意却佯装蔽惑，
我们不再形影不离而成陌路，
你的名字不再挂于我的口舌，
以免不经意对我们往日旧情叙说时
被我亵渎，将你的芳名辱没。

    为了你，我愿发誓要背叛自己，
    谁人你所恨，我就把他当仇敌！

090

Then hate me when thou wilt; if ever, now;

Now, while the world is bent my deeds to cross,

Join with the spite of fortune, make me bow,

And do not drop in for an after-loss:

Ah, do not, when my heart hath 'scap'd this sorrow,

Come in the rearward of a conquer'd woe;

Give not a windy night a rainy morrow,

To linger out a purpos'd overthrow.

If thou wilt leave me, do not leave me last,

When other petty griefs have done their spite,

But in the onset come; so shall I taste

At first the very worst of fortune's might,

 And other strains of woe, which now seem woe,

 Compared with loss of thee will not seem so.

090

你愿意恨我现在就开始恨吧，

反正世间所有人都同我作对，

你同厄运联手令我屈服自馁；

千万莫要等事后再乘人之危，

待我征服了痛苦又对我摧残，

切勿！那时我心已摆脱伤悲。

勿在一夜狂风后又密雨霏霏，

持续不断拖延存心将我击毁；

你若抛弃我，勿到剧终曲尾，

勿让那些小小悲伤作歹为非；

最好在开始就一股脑儿齐上，

让我先品尝最大厄运的滋味。

　　其他所有伤悲，看上去是伤悲，

　　　与失去你相比，可谓微乎其微。

091

Some glory in their birth, some in their skill,

Some in their wealth, some in their bodies' force,

Some in their garments, though new-fanglèd ill,

Some in their hawks and hounds, some in their horse;

And every humour hath his adjunct pleasure,

Wherein it finds a joy above the rest:

But these particulars are not my measure;

All these I better in one general best.

Thy love is better than high birth to me,

Richer than wealth, prouder than garments' cost,

Of more delight than hawks or horses be;

And having thee, of all men's pride I boast.

  Wretched in this alone, that thou mayst take

  All this away and me most wretched make.

091

有人因出身而夸耀，有人因学识而自豪，

有人因财富而标榜，有人因强壮而炫耀，

有人因风靡一时的奇装异服而昭彰，

有人因自己的猎鹰、猎犬和骏马而骄傲；

人们各自秉性不同，爱好也就各自相异，

且自认为是独一无二、盖世无双。

而以上这些没有一项是我的愿望，

我的快乐可远远把它们超越。

拥有你的爱远超过拥有高贵的出身，

远胜过拥有异装华服和万贯财富，

远超过拥有猎鹰、猎犬或骏骑；

只要拥有你，我将胜过天下人之荣光。

　　唯一不快乐是担心你把爱带走，

　　从而让我陷入弥亘无尽的哀愁。

092

But do thy worst to steal thyself away,

For term of life thou art assured mine,

And life no longer than thy love will stay,

For it depends upon that love of thine.

Then need I not to fear the worst of wrongs,

When in the least of them my life hath end.

I see a better state to me belongs

Than that which on thy humour doth depend;

Thou canst not vex me with inconstant mind,

Since that my life on thy revolt doth lie.

O, what a happy title do I find,

Happy to have thy love, happy to die!

    But what's so blessèd-fair that fears no blot?

    Thou mayst be false, and yet I know it not.

092

尽管你可以狠心地悄然离去，

但是你曾经对我许下终身。

我的生命不会长过你对我的爱，

因为你的爱是我生命的根基。

你对我稍有不满就可置我于死地，

我还何须惧怕这灭顶之击。

我找到了属于自己更好的归宿，

何须再对你唯唯诺诺、百顺百依。

既然你一变心我命都行将终结，

我何须再因你反复无常而忧虑。

你看，我为幸福找到了颠覆不破的理据：

拥有你的爱是幸福，你让我死也幸福至极。

　　可天下再甘美的情也会担心生嫌隙，

　　　你可能已有二心，只是我浑然不知。

093

So shall I live, supposing thou art true,

Like a deceivèd husband; so love's face

May still seem love to me, though alter'd new;

Thy looks with me, thy heart in other place.

For there can live no hatred in thine eye,

Therefore in that I cannot know thy change.

In many's looks the false heart's history

Is writ in moods and frowns and wrinkles strange,

But heaven in thy creation did decree

That in thy face sweet love should ever dwell;

Whate'er thy thoughts or thy heart's workings be,

Thy looks should nothing thence but sweetness tell.

  How like Eve's apple doth thy beauty grow,

  If thy sweet virtue answer not thy show!

093

于是我得像被骗的丈夫依然苟且，

假定你还依然对我忠贞不渝。

你脸上似乎依然对我泛着浓浓爱意，

尽管你情已别移，目光视我，心却远飞。

因为你眼中没有丝毫怨恨的神情，

所以我也难以觉察你情已移。

因为许多有情变史的人，

其脸上都明白标示：锁眉、蹙额、忧郁。

而上帝在造你身时就已决定，

让你脸上永驻甜美的浓浓爱意；

不论你内心思绪万端，情愫翻滚，

脸上总是挂着甘美的似水柔情。

　　如果你的品行与美质貌合神离，

　　那你的美貌与夏娃的苹果别无二致！

094

They that have power to hurt and will do none,

That do not do the thing they most do show,

Who, moving others, are themselves as stone,

Unmoved, cold, and to temptation slow,

They rightly do inherit heaven's graces

And husband nature's riches from expense;

They are the lords and owners of their faces,

Others but stewards of their excellence.

The summer's flower is to the summer sweet,

Though to itself it only live and die,

But if that flower with base infection meet,

The basest weed outbraves his dignity.

　　For sweetest things turn sourest by their deeds;

　　Lilies that fester smell far worse than weeds.

094

虽有伤人之力而无害人之举，

虽彰示最能为者而从来不为，

虽能打动别人而自己心静如水，

不动情愫，对诱惑漠然置之，

斯人应是承了上天的美质，

且精心呵护造物主所赐，免遭浪费，

他们是自己美貌的主人，

别人不过是其天资美质的管家。

夏日花朵虽然只是开谢交替，

却把夏天装扮得芬芳艳丽。

但是，若香花不幸染病，

即使最卑贱的杂草也比其高贵。

　　即使芳香四溢者，若自毁也臭不可闻，

　　百合花一旦腐烂便臭如杂草，不名一文。

095

How sweet and lovely dost thou make the shame

Which, like a canker in the fragrant rose,

Doth spot the beauty of thy budding name!

O, in what sweets dost thou thy sins enclose!

That tongue that tells the story of thy days,

Making lascivious comments on thy sport,

Cannot dispraise but in a kind of praise;

Naming thy name blesses an ill report.

O, what a mansion have those vices got

Which for their habitation chose out thee,

Where beauty's veil doth cover every blot,

And all things turn to fair that eyes can see!

    Take heed, dear heart, of this large privilege;

    The hardest knife ill-used doth lose his edge.

095

犹如把蛆虫藏在芳香四溢的玫瑰，

你把耻辱粉饰得如此可人娇美，

结果毁掉了你如花蕾初绽的美名！

你让你的罪过披上了美丽的外衣！

那张专门揭你轶闻趣事的大嘴，

把你的情爱说成是风流韵事，

以赞美之名行诋毁之实。

你的美名披在了恶名身上，

把你当成了它们的寓所，

为那些恶行筑起了殿堂，

里面的美丽纱幔把所有污垢掩藏，

使眼睛看到的一切都变得富丽堂皇。

　　我的心肝，你要珍重你的这种特权，

　　再锋利的刀刃，不当使用也会变钝。

096

Some say thy fault is youth, some wantonness;

Some say thy grace is youth and gentle sport;

Both grace and faults are lov'd of more and less;

Thou mak'st faults graces that to thee resort.

As on the finger of a thronèd queen

The basest jewel will be well esteem'd,

So are those errors that in thee are seen

To truths translated, and for true things deem'd

How many lambs might the stern wolf betray,

If like a lamb he could his looks translate!

How many gazers mighst thou lead away,

If thou wouldst use the strength of all thy state!

But do not so, I love thee such sort,

As thou being mine, mine is thy good report.

096

有人说你的过错是年少放浪，

有人说你的魅力是年少情长，

过错和魅力都有人赞赏，

你把过错也变成了魅力无疆。

犹如女王手指上佩戴的珠宝，

再粗劣也会受人仰望；

你的过错也与此相仿，

有人笃信为真，有人捧场作戏。

如果恶狼披上了羔羊的外衣，

那该会有多少羔羊遭殃！

如果你把你的魅力彰显无遗，

那该有多少人因你魂失魄靡！

　　切莫如此彰显，因为我无比爱你，

　　我拥有你，也要拥有你的美好名誉。

097

How like a winter hath my absence been

From thee, the pleasure of the fleeting year!

What freezings have I felt, what dark days seen!

What old December's bareness every where!

And yet this time remov'd was summer's time,

The teeming autumn, big with rich increase,

Bearing the wanton burden of the prime,

Like widow'd wombs after their lords' decease:

Yet this abundant issue seem'd to me

But hope of orphans and unfather'd fruit;

For summer and his pleasures wait on thee,

And, thou away, the very birds are mute;

    Or, if they sing, 'tis with so dull a cheer

    That leaves look pale, dreading the winter's near.

097

离开你的日子犹如严冬酷寒，

因为你就像飞逝流年中的一团温暖的火焰！

离开你，我心感到寒冷无比，眼前漆黑一片，

满目寒冬荒衰景，到处一派凄然！

可是我们分别却明明是在夏日炎炎，

虽说孕育着丰盈的秋天，

春天播下的种子将结出累累硕果，

可在我看来这繁盛的果实，

就像亡夫遗孀腹中的遗孤，

出生后没有父亲的呵护。

因为夏天和夏天的欢愉围绕在你身边，

你一离去连小鸟也缄口不再鸣啭。

　　即使它们鸣啭，声音也凄厉哀婉，

　　树叶也闻声失色，以为降临酷冬严寒。

098

From you have I been absent in the spring,

When proud-pied April dress'd in all his trim,

Hath put a spirit of youth in everything,

That heavy Saturn laugh'd and leap'd with him.

Yet nor the lays of birds nor the sweet smell

Of different flowers in odour and in hue

Could make me any summer's story tell,

Or from their proud lap pluck them where they grew.

Nor did I wonder at the lily's white,

Nor praise the deep vermilion in the rose;

They were but sweet, but figures of delight,

Drawn after you, you pattern of all those.

    Yet seem'd it winter still, and, you away,

    As with your shadow I with these did play.

098

你离开我是在明媚的春天，

大地披上了四月的彩妆绚烂，

万物焕发出青春的朝气，

就连沉重的土星①也欢呼雀跃。

不论是小鸟的动人的鸣唱，

还是绚丽多姿的百花芬芳，

都难让我说尽夏天的故事②，

也难让我采尽大地盛开的花枝。

我一点也不惊叹百合花的洁白，

也不赞叹玫瑰花的绯红艳丽。

它们芳香怡人，风姿百态，

无不都是模仿你——万美的模板。

　　　我似乎依然身在严冬，只缘你别离远去，

　　　我与百花嬉戏，宛如与你的身影相随相依。

---

① 在西方人眼中，土星象征着沉闷、忧郁。——译者注

② 夏天的故事：欢乐的故事。莎士比亚时代总是视夏天为美好，另参见莎士比亚十四行诗

　　第十八首《我可否把你比作夏日绮丽》。——译者注

099

The forward violet thus did I chide:

Sweet thief, whence didst thou steal thy sweet that smells,

If not from my love's breath? The purple pride

Which on thy soft cheek for complexion dwells

In my love's veins thou hast too grossly dyed.

The lily I condemnèd for thy hand,

And buds of marjoram had stol'n thy hair;

The roses fearfully on thorns did stand,

One blushing shame, another white despair;

A third, nor red nor white, had stol'n of both

And to his robbery had annex'd thy breath;

But, for his theft, in pride of all his growth

A vengeful canker eat him up to death.

More flowers I not'd, yet I none could see

But sweet or colour it had stol'n from thee.

099

于是我曾责问早开的紫罗兰^①：

"温柔的小偷，你芳香四溢，

还不是从吾爱那里盗取？

涂抹在你冰肌玉颜上的嫣红绛紫，

还不是在吾爱的血管中浸渍？"

我谴责百合花偷了你玉手之白皙，

我谴责墨角兰花蕾偷了你头发之秀美；

至于荆刺满身的玫瑰站在那里瑟瑟发抖，

其中，红的盗你娇羞，白的盗你的忧愁，

红白相间者既盗娇羞，也盗忧愁，

还把你的香馨偷去漫洒于娇羞与忧愁。

因其行窃之时恰值其花盛放，

复仇的蛆虫便将其蛀蚀而亡。

　　我见过鲜花万紫千红，但没见过哪一种

　　不是从你那里盗窃秀色和芳香而长成。

---

① 此诗比十四行诗多了一行，其中第一行为导语。——译者注

100

Where art thou, Muse, that thou forget'st so long

To speak of that which gives thee all thy might?

Spend'st thou thy fury on some worthless song,

Dark'ning thy pow'r to lend base subjects light?

Return, forgetful Muse, and straight redeem

In gentle numbers time so idly spent;

Sing to the ear that doth thy lays esteem

And gives thy pen both skill and argument.

Rise, resty Muse, my love's sweet face survey,

If Time have any wrinkle graven there;

If any, be a satire to decay,

And make Time's spoils despis'd everywhere.

   Give my love fame faster than Time wastes life;

   So thou prevent'st his scythe and crook'd knife.

100

我的诗神，你到底去了何方？

这么久忘记了讴歌吾爱，

他可是赋予了你无穷的力量。

干嘛倾诗情于无价值的吟唱

消耗精力于那些低俗的题材上？

归来吧，健忘的诗神，将功补过，

写出柔美的诗章，弥补虚度的时光，

为敬仰你并给你灵感和艺技的人而歌唱！

醒来吧，懒惰的诗神，看看时间老人

是否在吾爱的脸上刻下道道皱纹？

如果是的话，快写诗挖苦那致衰鬼，

让时间暴君的掠美行动处处遭人鄙夷。

　　快！在时间暴君戕害吾爱生命前将其美名颂扬，

　　如此，你就可以将时间暴君风刀霜剑彻底抵挡！

101

O truant Muse, what shall be thy amends

For thy neglect of truth in beauty dyed?

Both truth and beauty on my love depends;

So dost thou too, and therein dignified.

Make answer, Muse: wilt thou not haply say,

"Truth needs no colour, with his colour fix'd,

Beauty no pencil, beauty's truth to lay;

But best is best, if never intermix'd?"

Because he needs no praise, wilt thou be dumb?

Excuse not silence so; for 't lies in thee

To make him much outlive a gildèd tomb,

And to be praised of ages yet to be.

     Then do thy office, Muse; I teach thee how

     To make him seem long hence as he shows now.

101

你对以美浸真心不在焉、玩岁愒日，

你将如何加以弥补，我懒惰的诗神？

真和美从来都与吾爱形影相随，

你也应靠吾爱获得仰慕和敬重。

你或许会做出这样回答：

"真有其本色，无须为其增光添彩，

美有其本真，无须为其涂脂抹粉，

不加任何粉饰，才是至美至真。"

难道他无须赞美，你就默不作声？

切勿为你沉默寻找借口，

你能让他比镀金的墓碑更长存，

能让他在将来被人永远赞颂。

　　　诗神，那就尽忠职守吧，我会教你

　　　如何让他流芳百世，依然像今天这样风姿绰丽。

102

My love is strengthen'd, though more weak in seeming;

I love not less, though less the show appear.

That love is merchandiz'd whose rich esteeming

The owner's tongue doth publish everywhere.

Our love was new and then but in the spring

When I was wont to greet it with my lays.

As Philomel in summer's front doth sing

And stops her pipe in growth of riper days.

Not that the summer is less pleasant now

Than when her mournful hymns did hush the night.

But that wild music burthens every bough

And sweets grown common lose their dear delight.

    Therefore, like her, I sometime hold my tongue,

    Because I would not dull you with my song.

102

我对你的爱愈是强烈，看上去愈平静如水，

我爱你与日俱增，脸上却不动声色。

爱若被作为商品打上价签，

只有贪财的持有者才聒噪地四处宣扬。

我们的爱始于一个明媚的春天，

彼时我习惯用歌为我们的爱欢呼，

宛如夜莺在初夏鸣啭歌唱，

直至万物繁盛成熟才息声。

这并非因夏日比春天缺少了欢乐，

而是因为她哀婉的啼声让暗夜陷入寂静。

尔后百鸟齐聚枝头狂鸣，

悦耳动听的鸣啭若习以为常，魅力也会被消靡。

    因此，我就像夜莺那样有时缄口沉默，

    因为我不想用我习以为常的歌声令你感到乏味。

103

Alack, what poverty my Muse brings forth,

That having such a scope to show her pride,

The argument, all bare, is of more worth

Than when it hath my added praise beside!

O, blame me not, if I no more can write!

Look in your glass, and there appears a face

That over-goes my blunt invention quite,

Dulling my lines and doing me disgrace.

Were it not sinful, then, striving to mend,

To mar the subject that before was well?

For to no other pass my verses tend

Than of your graces and your gifts to tell;

    And more, much more, than in my verse can sit

    Your own glass shows you when you look in it.

103

我的诗神本可一展诗艺风采，

就是因为增加了我画蛇添足的赞美，

反倒不如其题材自身精深高妙，

结果却呈献出如此平庸的诗篇！

噢，如果我不善写诗也切莫责怪我。

请照照镜子吧，镜中的面孔

远胜过我的平庸诗作挖空心思对你的描摹，

让我的诗相形见绌，令我颜面尽失。

本想锦上添花，却把美诗主题辱没，

这难道不是一种不可饶恕的罪过？

除了写你的美质和天资，

我的诗却显得词穷句竭、毫无文采。

　　你照照镜子，镜中你的形象，

　　远胜过我的庸诗对你的赞扬。

104

To me, fair friend, you never can be old,

For as you were when first your eye I eyed,

Such seems your beauty still. Three winters cold

Have from the forests shook three summers' pride,

Three beauteous springs to yellow autumn turn'd

In process of the seasons have I seen,

Three April perfumes in three hot Junes burn'd,

Since first I saw you fresh, which yet are green.

Ah! yet doth beauty, like a dial-hand,

Steal from his figure and no pace perceiv'd;

So your sweet hue, which methinks still doth stand,

Hath motion and mine eye may be deceiv'd.

    For fear of which, hear this, thou age unbred:

    Ere you were born was beauty's summer dead.

104

美丽的朋友，你在我眼中永远不会老，

自从我和你第一次双眸相遇，

至今你依然美丽如初。

严冬已三度摇落盛夏芳林的妖娆，

芳春已三度变为寒秋的枯色荒景，

四月的芳菲也已三度被六月的骄阳焚烧，

只看到季节的更替轮回，

你却依然像我初见时那样美丽清新，

啊，美质就像时钟的指针，

不觉脚步匆匆，时光悄然流逝。

我以为你美丽的风采永驻，

却也在悄悄消逝，只是我的眼睛被蒙蔽。

　　我怀着万分恐惧毅然告诉后世：

　　　你们尚未出世，芳夏就已枯靡。

105

Let not my love be call'd idolatry,

Nor my belovèd as an idol show,

Since all alike my songs and praises be

To one, of one, still such, and ever so.

Kind is my love to-day, to-morrow kind,

Still constant in a wondrous excellence;

Therefore my verse, to constancy confin'd,

One thing expressing, leaves out difference.

"Fair, kind and true," is all my argument,

"Fair, kind, and true" varying to other words;

And in this change is my invention spent,

Three themes in one, which wondrous scope affords.

    "Fair, kind, and true," have often lived alone,

    Which three, till now, never kept seat in one.

105

切莫把我的爱说成是对偶像的崇拜，

也勿将吾爱看做壁龛里的神像一尊。

既然我的颂歌和赞词都献给一人，

所以主题都一以贯之，永不变调。

吾爱今日善良，明日也善良，

恒久不变，恪守始终，

所以吾诗主题也一以贯之。

高扬一个主题：歌颂真善美。

真善美是我全部的诗心，

真善美是我异曲同工的全部诗句。

词虽变幻无穷，诗心坚守如一，任诗才驰骋，

三个主题合一，为我的诗作开辟了更广阔的前景。

  　真善美从来各自特立独行，

  　而今集一人之身相辅相成。

106

When in the chronicle of wasted time

I see descriptions of the fairest wights,

And beauty making beautiful old rhyme

In praise of ladies dead and lovely knights,

Then, in the blazon of sweet beauty's best,

Of hand, of foot, of lip, of eye, of brow,

I see their antique pen would have express'd

Even such a beauty as you master now.

So all their praises are but prophecies

Of this our time, all you prefiguring;

And, for they look'd but with divining eyes,

They had not skill enough your worth to sing:

    For we, which now behold these present days,

    Had eyes to wonder, but lack tongues to praise.

106

当我潜心研读远古历史典籍时，

看到俊男靓女的奇闻轶事。

古诗之所以美是因为它歌颂的就是美——

美色绝伦的淑女和风流倜傥的骑士。

从歌颂绝代佳人的诗章

对美人手足双唇双眼双眉的赞美

可以看到古代诗人恰是要颂扬

诚如你今天所展现的美质。

因此他们的颂歌就是预言，

预言了我们这个时代，预言了你的美丽风采。

不过，由于他们仅用预测的眼光审视，

所以缺少精湛的艺术来歌颂你的无价美质。

　　　就连当今的我们，虽有幸一睹你的尊容，

　　　也只是望而兴叹，却无诗才来把你赞颂。

107

Not mine own fears, nor the prophetic soul
Of the wide world dreaming on things to come,
Can yet the lease of my true love control,
Suppos'd as forfeit to a confin'd doom.
The mortal moon hath her eclipse endur'd
And the sad augurs mock their own presage;
Incertainties now crown themselves assur'd
And peace proclaims olives of endless age.
Now with the drops of this most balmy time
My love looks fresh, and death to me subscribes,
Since, spite of him, I'll live in this poor rhyme,
While he insults o'er dull and speechless tribes.
    And thou in this shalt find thy monument,
    When tyrants' crests and tombs of brass are spent.

107

无论我担忧的内心，还是先知的灵魂，

都不能为我忠贞的爱定下期限，

哪怕先知能预测人间未来事物的发生与消亡，

尽管人们都认为爱情终将葬入坟墓。

人间的月亮已度过她的月蚀①，

悲观占卜家的预言却成了笑柄②；

重重疑云代之以天下太平，

宣示和平的橄榄枝将万世长青。

如今沐浴着太平盛世的甘露，

吾爱更展新容，死神也对我称臣屈从。

尽管死神敢把沉默无声者③欺凌，

却对我无可奈何，因为我可借诗永生。

　　　即使暴君的勋徽和铜塑已灰飞烟灭，

　　　你的丰碑依旧巍然屹立在我的诗中。

---

① 人间的月亮，喻指伊丽莎白一世女王。度过她的月蚀，意指度过危险时刻。——译者注

② 有人预言伊丽莎白一世驾崩后会天下大乱，预言未果，当成为笑柄。——译者注

③ 沉默无声者：指不著诗文的普通众生。——译者注

108

What's in the brain that ink may character

Which hath not figur'd to thee my true spirit?

What's new to speak, what new to register,

That may express my love or thy dear merit?

Nothing, sweet boy; but yet, like prayers divine,

I must each day say o'er the very same,

Counting no old thing old, thou mine, I thine,

Even as when first I hallow'd thy fair name.

So that eternal love in love's fresh case

Weighs not the dust and injury of age,

Nor gives to necessary wrinkles place,

But makes antiquity for aye his page;

    Finding the first conceit of love there bred

    Where time and outward form would show it dead.

108

我脑海里的思绪只要能变成诗文，

无一不是向你表达我的真心！

还有什么新的琼词妙语

能赞颂你的美，表达我的情？

没有，我的爱，我会像做祷告一样，

弥日亘时地一遍遍诵读同样的经文。

诵读复诵读：你属于我，我属于你，

正如当初我重复呼唤你神圣的芳名。

如此，永恒的爱穿上爱的新装，

再不用担忧岁月的侵蚀和尘埃的浸涴，

额头也不给皱纹爬上留下空隙，

虽然为旧调，却依然会谱出新篇。

> 在岁月与外貌使爱看上去衰靡之处，

> 却发现依然不断孕育着初恋时对爱的遐想。

109

O, never say that I was false of heart,

Though absence seem'd my flame to qualify.

As easy might I from myself depart

As from my soul which in thy breast doth lie:

That is my home of love; if I have rang'd,

Like him that travels I return again,

Just to the time, not with the time exchang'd,

So that myself bring water for my stain.

Never believe, though in my nature reign'd

All frailties that besiege all kinds of blood,

That it could so preposterously be stain'd,

To leave for nothing all thy sum of good;

    For nothing this wide universe I call,

    Save thou, my rose; in it thou art my all.

109

噢，切莫说我曾对你假意虚情，

尽管分别似乎使我的激情变得平静。

我不能抛开自己的肉体，

犹如我不能离开寄居你心房的灵魂，

你的心房是我情之所寄的家园。

假如我曾经出走浪迹天涯，

现在如远游的浪子准时归家，

且并未因久别而心生变故。

于是我自带洁水①洗涤我的污迹。

虽然我天性有人类所具有的一切弱点，

但切勿以为我愚蠢得无可理喻，

以至于为虚无缥缈而抛弃你这稀世奇珍。

  我把这浩瀚的宇宙视为虚无缥缈，

  只有你，我的玫瑰，才是我的整个宇宙！

---

① 这里指眼泪。——译者注

110

Alas,'tis true I have gone here and there

And made myself a motley to the view,

Gor'd mine own thoughts, sold cheap what is most dear,

Made old offences of affections new;

Most true it is that I have look'd on truth

Askance and strangely, But, by all above,

These blenches gave my heart another youth,

And worse essays prov'd thee my best of love.

Now all is done, have what shall have no end.

Mine appetite I never more will grind

On newer proof, to try an older friend,

A god in love, to whom I am confined.

  Then give me welcome, next my heaven the best,

  Even to thy pure and most most loving breast.

110

唉，我的确曾东走西奔，

还在大庭广众下演过小丑，

自尊心受到极大伤害，鬼使神差地把珍宝贱卖，

为结交新友，不惜获咎故友；

我的确曾以不屑的目光怀疑真情。

不过，我可以对着苍天吐真言，

尽管结新欢又让我春心荡漾，

但这错误尝试证明你才是我至爱至真。

往事已去，请接受我爱意无尽，

我绝不会再让我的爱火蔓延。

以结交新友考验旧友，最终证明：

你是我的爱神，我的爱弥久不离你身。

　　迎接我吧，我的第二天堂，

　　迎接我入你纯洁无瑕、至爱无疆的心房。

111

O, for my sake do you with Fortune chide,

The guilty goddess of my harmful deeds,

That did not better for my life provide

Than public means which public manners breeds.

Thence comes it that my name receives a brand,

And almost thence my nature is subdued

To what it works in, like the dyer's hand.

Pity me then and wish I were renew'd;

Whilst, like a willing patient, I will drink

Potions of eisel 'gainst my strong infection:

No bitterness that I will bitter think,

Nor double penance, to correct correction.

    Pity me then, dear friend, and I assure ye

    Even that your pity is enough to cure me.

111

啊，为了我你要把命运女神责难，

正是她导致我的行为不端。

她不安排我过上富裕生活，

却让我混同草民度日谋生。

最终让我背上了蒙羞的恶名，

像染工的手一样被玷污，

还扼杀了我本有的天性。

怜悯我吧，愿我能获新生，

我会像恪遵医嘱的病人，

喝下一剂剂醋药①治疗我的痼疾，

不管它有多苦我也要一饮而尽，

为治顽疾，我也不怕剂量加倍。

　　怜悯我吧，我的挚友，我敢保证，

　　您的怜悯足以治好我的痼疾顽症。

---

① 莎士比亚时代的英国人认为醋可以治病防疫。这里当然是喻用。——译者注

112

Your love and pity doth the impression fill

Which vulgar scandal stamp'd upon my brow;

For what care I who calls me well or ill,

So you o'er-green my bad, my good allow?

You are my all the world, and I must strive

To know my shames and praises from your tongue;

None else to me, nor I to none alive,

That my steel'd sense or changes right or wrong.

In so profound abysm I throw all care

Of others' voices, that my adder's sense

To critic and to flatterer stoppèd are.

Mark how with my neglect I do dispense:

    You are so strongly in my purpose bred,

    That all the world besides methinks are dead.

112

请用你的爱和怜悯除去我额头上的烙印，

那是流言蜚语给我烙上的污痕。

只要你之于我激短扬长、心照神交，

我何须还在意众人的说长道短？

你就是我的整个世界，

我必须听到你亲口对我的褒贬。

之于世界我已死，我视世界业已亡，

只有你能感化我或善或恶的铁石心肠。

别人的品头论足我都抛在脑后，

充耳不闻，犹如聋聩的蝰蛇，

不管他们是吹毛求疵还是恶意奉承。

我之所以这样对别人的品评漠视与超然，

　　　只缘你深深地植根于我的心田，

　　　在我看来，除你之外这个世界已长眠。

113

Since I left you, mine eye is in my mind;

And that which governs me to go about

Doth part his function and is partly blind,

Seems seeing, but effectually is out;

For it no form delivers to the heart

Of bird, of flower, or shape, which it doth latch:

Of his quick objects hath the mind no part,

Nor his own vision holds what it doth catch:

For if it see the rud'st or gentlest sight,

The most sweet favour or deformed'st creature,

The mountain or the sea, the day or night,

The crow or dove, it shapes them to your feature.

 Incapable of more, replete with you,

 My most true mind thus makes mine eye untrue.

113

在我离开你后我的眼睛便深居心宫，

此前它指挥我四处漂泊巡行。

如今它像良弓深藏，有些失灵，

看上去在凝望，实际已分神。

因为小鸟花草在眼前掠过，

其模样却不能传到我内心。

心宫也就无法分享眼前的图景，

而眼睛自己又不能将其留存。

它看到的景色不论最俗还是最雅，

看到的面孔不论是最丑还是最美，

所见不论是高山还是大海，是白天还是黑夜，

不论是乌鸦还是白鸽，都将化作你的倩影，

　　　因为满心里都是你，使他物无容置身，

　　　正是我真诚的心让我的眼睛视觉失真。

114

Or whether doth my mind, being crown'd with you,

Drink up the monarch's plague, this flattery?

Or whether shall I say, mine eye saith true,

And that your love taught it this alchemy,

To make of monsters and things indigest

Such cherubins as your sweet self resemble,

Creating every bad a perfect best

As fast as objects to his beams assemble?

O, 'tis the first; 'tis flattery in my seeing,

And my great mind most kingly drinks it up;

Mine eye well knows what with his gust is 'greeing,

And to his palate doth prepare the cup.

    If it be poison'd, 'tis the lesser sin

    That mine eye loves it and doth first begin.

114

我的心把你当至高无上的皇冠加冕后

是否染上了帝王病——喜欢别人阿谀奉承？

还是说我的眼睛告诉的的确是实情，

因为你的爱让它学会了点石成金的法术，

让魑魅魍魉也能化成天使——

像你一样美丽可爱、典雅温柔；

无论如何丑陋的东西，

只要遇上它的目光就会变得完美无比？

不，而是前者，是我的眼睛在献媚，

而我伟大的心却一吞而进。

我的眼睛深知我心的好恶，

便完全按其口味准备汤羹。

　　即使汤羹有毒，眼睛也非罪不可赦，

　　因为是眼睛爱之在前，且先尝为敬。

115

Those lines that I before have writ do lie,

Even those that said I could not love you dearer;

Yet then my judgment knew no reason why

My most full flame should afterwards burn clearer.

But reckoning time, whose million'd accidents

Creep in 'twixt vows and change decrees of kings,

Tan sacred beauty, blunt the sharp'st intents,

Divert strong minds to the course of altering things;

Alas, why, fearing of time's tyranny,

Might I not then say, "Now I love you best,"

When I was certain o'er incertainty,

Crowning the present, doubting of the rest?

　　Love is a babe; then might I not say so,

　　To give full growth to that which still doth grow?

115

我以前写的诗章其实都是在撒谎，

甚至也包括那些说爱你至极的诗行。

那时我见识短浅，说不清是什么原因

让我的炽热的情火怎么会越烧越旺。

哪料想，时间暴君千万次撕毁誓约，

篡改圣旨，变佳丽为丑女，挫败壮志雄心，

就算你意志坚强，甚至坚不可摧，

你最终也要屈从时间暴君对万物的不断更替；

彼时，我爱笃定，而天道无常，

虽然对当下豪情满怀，却对未来充满惆怅，

唉！既然害怕时间暴君的专横，

我当时为什么不说"现在我爱你至极"？

　　爱是个婴儿，因此那时我不可能口出此言，

　　为的是让这正在成长的婴儿发育至臻成熟。

116

Let me not to the marriage of true minds

Admit impediments. Love is not love

Which alters when it alteration finds,

Or bends with the remover to remove:

O, no, it is an ever-fixed mark

That looks on tempests and is never shaken;

It is the star to every wandering bark,

Whose worth's unknown, although his height be taken.

Love's not Time's fool, though rosy lips and cheeks

Within his bending sickle's compass come;

Love alters not with his brief hours and weeks,

But bears it out even to the edge of doom.

    If this be error and upon me proved,

    I never writ, nor no man ever loved.

116

我不认为有情人终成眷属会有障碍，

那种见异思迁的情根本不是真情，

那种随风转舵的爱根本不是真爱。

爱是海上安若磐石的灯塔，

面对暴风雨狂袭岿然屹立。

爱是茫茫海上航船的指路明灯，

尽管你可测定其高几何，

但是无法估量其值无穷。

爱不是时间暴君愚弄的玩偶，

尽管冰肌玉颜难逃其风刀霜剑。

爱不仅在朝朝暮暮的卿卿我我，

更在历久弥坚的厮守，直到地老天荒。

　　　　如果有谁证明我是在痴人说梦，

　　　　我永不再写爱这一主题，权作人间无爱无情。

117

Accuse me thus: that I have scanted all

Wherein I should your great deserts repay,

Forgot upon your dearest love to call,

Whereto all bonds do tie me day by day;

That I have frequent been with unknown minds,

And given to time your own dear-purchas'd right;

That I have hoisted sail to all the winds

Which should transport me farthest from your sight.

Book both my wilfulness and errors down,

And on just proof surmise accumulate;

Bring me within the level of your frown,

But shoot not at me in your waken'd hate;

    Since my appeal says I did strive to prove

    The constancy and virtue of your love.

117

你就尽情地骂我薄情寡义吧，

骂我未能对你的恩德予以报答，

把你给予的至爱忘得一无所遗，

尽管我弥日亘时对你情思紧系；

骂我盲目频频结交陌路，

因辜负了你一往深情而负韶华；

骂我不管东风西风都扬帆，

只为起航远行离你遥远到天涯。

那就记下我的刚愎自用和过错吧，

以积累证据来证明你的猜忌；

你可以叫我到你面前看你的生气的脸色，

但切莫向我射出仇恨飞箭让我毙命，

　　　因为我要争辩说：我这样才证实

　　　你对我的爱忠贞不渝、高尚无比！

118

Like as, to make our appetites more keen,

With eager compounds we our palate urge,

As, to prevent our maladies unseen,

We sicken to shun sickness when we purge,

Even so, being full of your ne'er-cloying sweetness,

To bitter sauces did I frame my feeding,

And, sick of welfare, found a kind of meetness

To be diseased ere that there was true needing.

Thus policy in love, t' anticipate

The ills that were not, grew to faults assured,

And brought to medicine a healthful state

Which, rank of goodness, would by ill be cured:

    But thence I learn, and find the lesson true,

    Drugs poison him that so fell sick of you.

118

正如我们为了增强食欲

常用辛辣调料来刺激味觉一样，

我们为预防疾病须吃泻药①。

同样，饱尝了那从不厌腻的甘甜，

我转而品尝苦味；

甚至，厌倦了健康，

觉得生生病也未尝不可，

尽管实际上并不需要生病。

这种本来为防病的情场小伎俩

往往却弄假成真②。

原本体魄健康却令其吃药——

好端端的康体却用病来医治。

　　　　但我却因此得到启示：谁因爱情犯了病③，

　　　　如果用药医治，其毒性比病本身还要重。

---

① 莎士比亚时代的英国认为吃泻药能防病。——译者注

② 全诗用隐喻手法叙写爱情剪不断、理还乱的郁结情态。——译者注

③ 这里指因迷恋某人而产生的相思病。——译者注

119

What potions have I drunk of Siren tears,

Distill'd from limbecks foul as hell within,

Applying fears to hopes and hopes to fears,

Still losing when I saw myself to win!

What wretch'd errors hath my heart committed,

Whilst it hath thought itself so blessed never!

How have mine eyes out of their spheres been fitted

In the distraction of this madding fever!

O benefit of ill! Now I find true

That better is by evil still made better;

And ruin'd love, when it is built anew,

Grows fairer than at first, more strong, far greater.

    So I return rebuk'd to my content,

    And gain by ill thrice more than I have spent.

119

我不知道喝过多少塞壬①的眼泪——

犹如来自地狱蒸馏锅的污液，

使我在恐惧中怀着希望，试图以希望消弭恐惧，

满以为胜利在望，却依然绝望重重！

内心满以为沉浸在从未有过的幸福，

眼球几乎要从眼眶一跃而出。

我心醉神迷至疯狂昏聩！

殊不知却犯下了严重的错误。

不过，正如常言所说，祸兮福所倚。

我发现事情经过磨砺才会好上加好，

如果被毁的爱破镜重圆，

会变得更美、更弥坚、更辉煌！

　　　所以我虽受责罚，但却心满意足，

　　　只缘我因祸得福，福报远超悲苦。

---

① 塞壬（Siren）：希腊神话中半人半鸟的女海妖，惯以动人歌声迷惑航海者触礁。——译
者注

120

That you were once unkind befriends me now,

And for that sorrow, which I then did feel,

Needs must I under my transgression bow,

Unless my nerves were brass or hammer's steel.

For if you were by my unkindness shaken,

As I by yours, you've pass'd a hell of time;

And I, a tyrant, have no leisure taken

To weigh how once I suffer'd in your crime.

O, that our night woe might have remember'd

My deepest sense, how hard true sorrow hits,

And soon to you, as you to me, then tender'd

The humble salve which wounded bosoms fits!

But that your trespass now becomes a fee;

Mine ransoms yours, and must ransom me.

120

你过去对我无情如今却使我受益，

想到当时自己因你无情而痛苦不堪，

我现在就不能对你薄情寡义，

除非我是个铁石心肠的无情之人。

如果我也像你对我一样对你无义无情，

你也会深受打击，经历犹如在地狱般的楚痛；

我这个刚愎自用的痴情狂，

不想费时计较你的罪过使我遭受了怎样的折磨。

噢，但愿那充满忧郁的暗夜不致使我忘记

给我心灵深处造成的何等打击；

但我也会像你对我一样对你报以柔情——表达歉疚——

这是一剂良药，能治愈心灵的无限伤痛！

　　如今，你的过失却成了一笔赎金——，

　　使我原谅了你的过失；你对我也应宽容。

121

'Tis better to be vile than vile esteem'd,

When not to be receives reproach of being,

And the just pleasure lost which is so deem'd

Not by our feeling but by others' seeing.

For why should others, false adulterate eyes

Give salutation to my sportive blood?

Or on my frailties why are frailer spies,

Which in their wills count bad what I think good?

No, I am that I am, and they that level

At my abuses reckon up their own.

I may be straight, though they themselves be bevel;

By their rank thoughts my deeds must not be shown;

Unless this general evil they maintain,

All men are bad, and in their badness reign.

121

如果高洁反被诬为卑鄙而背负恶名，

与其被人诬蔑为恶倒不如索性去为恶；

原本是正当的欢情却因被冠上恶名而终——

全凭臆测，而非凭我们情感来断定。

虚伪淫荡的眼睛有什么理由

对我天性的情爱投以怀疑的神情？

自己满身瑕玷为什么却总盯着我的弱点，

为什么我认为善者，他们却反认为是恶？

我问心无愧，他们对我恶言诽谤，

只能证明他们自己内心的肮脏。

我堂堂正正，他们却心污行秽，

他们居心叵测怎能来评判我的光明磊落？

　　　　除非他们认定世人皆邪恶，

　　　　把人间正道歪曲为无恶不作。

122

Thy gift, thy tables, are within my brain
Full character'd with lasting memory,
Which shall above that idle rank remain
Beyond all date, even to eternity;
Or at the least, so long as brain and heart
Have faculty by nature to subsist;
Till each to raz'd oblivion yield his part
Of thee, thy record never can be miss'd.
That poor retention could not so much hold,
Nor need I tallies thy dear love to score;
Therefore to give them from me was I bold,
To trust those tables that receive thee more.
　　To keep an adjunct to remember thee
　　Were to import forgetfulness in me.

122

你送给我的礼物①我一刻也没忘记，

上面写满了难以忘怀的温情回忆，

它们弥足珍贵，胜过一切赠言寄语，

而且将历久弥长，直到永远；

至少说，只要人脑思维不止，

只要人心跳动不息，

心脑二者都不会把你忘记，

有关你的记录就不会被遗弃。

但是那可怜的手册记不下你万丈深情。

我又不想将你的挚情另册记录，

便冒昧地不再使用你送的手册续记，

而将其寄托给更好的地方——我的诗里。

　　如果借助旁物才能把你铭记，

　　那岂不在说我心里没有你？

---

① 该礼物是一本手册。——译者注

123

No, Time, thou shalt not boast that I do change:

Thy pyramids built up with newer might

To me are nothing novel, nothing strange;

They are but dressings of a former sight.

Our dates are brief, and therefore we admire

What thou dost foist upon us that is old,

And rather make them born to our desire

Than think that we before have heard them told.

Thy registers and thee I both defy,

Not wondering at the present nor the past,

For thy records and what we see doth lie,

Made more or less by thy continual haste.

    This I do vow and this shall ever be;

    I will be true, despite thy scythe and thee.

123

时间老人，你休夸口说我会随你改变，
即使你力量无穷能把金字塔重新筑起，
这对我来说一点也不感意外、不觉新奇，
它们只不过是旧景披上了新衣。
因为生命短暂，所以世间众生才对你
强加的旧货色表现出歆羡，
你甚至把旧货当做人们向往之物来出品，
却不成想人们早已对其传遍街头巷尾。
对你和你所做的记载我都从心里蔑视，
对当今和往昔我都不觉得有什么惊奇，
因为你的记载和我们所见都不足为信，
全都是你匆匆脚步留下的足迹。
　　我现在郑重发誓，而且永不食言：
　　你的镰刀再锋利，我也会始终如一。

124

If my dear love were but the child of state,

It might for Fortune's bastard be unfather'd,

As subject to Time's love or to Time's hate,

Weeds among weeds, or flowers with flowers gather'd.

No, it was buildèd far from accident;

It suffers not in smiling pomp, nor falls

Under the blow of thrallèd discontent,

Whereto the inviting time our fashion calls.

It fears not policy, that heretic,

Which works on leases of short-number'd hours,

But all alone stands hugely politic,

That it nor grows with heat nor drowns with showers.

 To this I witness call the fools of Time,

 Which die for goodness, who have liv'd for crime.

124

假如我对你的挚爱是时势之子，

那就是命运的私生子而没有父亲，

爱恨完全看时间暴君的好恶：

可能贱如莠草，也可能贵如香花。

但是，我对你的爱绝非时势之子，绝不受时势支配，

既不会因身处浮华顺境而有丝毫减弱，

也不会因逆境失意遭打击而颓靡不振——

这个诱人的时代要吾辈面对逆境、正视挫折。

我对你的爱不惧奸佞权谋，

因为权谋只能短时得逞。

我的爱则超然屹立，且深识远虑，

顺境不骄，逆境不馁。

　　我要传唤那些时间的玩偶来对此作见证：

　　那些一生作恶多端的人，到死时却想从善而终。

125

Were 't aught to me I bore the canopy,

With my extern the outward honouring,

Or laid great bases for eternity,

Which prove more short than waste or ruining?

Have I not seen dwellers on form and favour

Lose all, and more, by paying too much rent,

For compound sweet forgoing simple savour,

Pitiful thrivers, in their gazing spent?

No, let me be obsequious in thy heart,

And take thou my oblation, poor but free,

Which is not mix'd with seconds, knows no art,

But mutual render, only me for thee.

    Hence, thou suborn'd informer! A true soul

    When most impeach'd stands least in thy control.

125

高擎华盖为表面荣光，

筑基固本为万古流芳，

结果一切却瞬间飞逝，顷刻消亡，

这又有何用场？

曾见华贵房客威奢荣光，

最终倾其所有难付房租高昂。

可怜的富人弃简约而求表面华贵风光，

耗尽心血于攀附权贵上。

我则不然，我把无限的虔敬留在你心中，

请收下我这绵薄而由衷供奉，

它无丝毫掺假，也无任何城府，

纯属我对你的厚德报恩。

　　噢！你们这些心存偏见的诽谤者，快滚开吧，

　　真挚的心面对你们的诽谤会岿然屹立！

126

O thou, my lovely boy, who in thy power

Dost hold Time's fickle glass, his sickle, hour;

Who hast by waning grown, and therein show'st

Thy lovers withering as thy sweet self grow'st!

If Nature, sovereign mistress over wrack,

As thou goest onwards, still will pluck thee back,

She keeps thee to this purpose, that her skill

May time disgrace and wretched minutes kill.

Yet fear her, O thou minion of her pleasure!

She may detain, but not still keep, her treasure.

Her audit, though delay'd, answer'd must be,

And her quietus is to render thee.

126①

你控制了时间君的沙漏和风刀霜剑，
我的爱，你可真是威力无边！
随着时光飞逝，你的爱友不断凋萎，
你却愈发光彩照人、活力年轻！
你在生命的征途上阔步前行，
造物主这位女王却将你拖回，
让你保持年轻，以此炫耀她的法力——
可以让时间君蒙羞，杀退分秒，让时间倒流。
你这个造物主的宠儿，可要对她提防！
她的宝贝仅可暂留而不能永存，
她的欠债，可延期但终要偿清，
届时她为偿债肯定要把你还回。

---

① 这首诗原诗只有十二行，且韵律安排也不同于十四行诗的制式。——译者注

127

In the old age black was not counted fair,

Or if it were, it bore not beauty's name;

But now is black beauty's successive heir,

And beauty slander'd with a bastard shame.

For since each hand hath put on nature's power,

Fairing the foul with art's false borrow'd face,

Sweet beauty hath no name, no holy bower,

But is profan'd, if not lives in disgrace.

Therefore my mistress' eyes are raven black,

Her eyes so suited, and they mourners seem

At such, who, not born fair, no beauty lack,

Slandering creation with a false esteem.

    Yet so they mourn, becoming of their woe,

    That every tongue says beauty should look so.

127

旧时黑色从不被视为娇媚，

就算娇媚也不被算在美的行列。

如今黑色承袭了美的合法名分，

由此其美遭谗害，被冠私生子之名，无端蒙羞。

自从世人的双手获得了自然的功力，

便可通过描眉搽粉，借假面来把丑美化，

于是美就失去了名分和神圣的闺房，

就算不再受人羞辱，也遭人轻蔑。

而我的情人有一对浓黑的眼眉，

眼睛也和双眉一样乌黑，像个哭丧女

在感伤那些先天丑陋却后天炫美的人，

他们用虚美玷污了造物主的功力。

　　　她双眼哀愁，透出一种伤感的娴雅，

　　　而人们都说，美本该就是这般模样。

128

How oft, when thou, my music, music play'st,

Upon that blessed wood whose motion sounds

With thy sweet fingers, when thou gently sway'st

The wiry concord that mine ear confounds,

Do I envy those jacks that nimble leap

To kiss the tender inward of thy hand,

Whilst my poor lips, which should that harvest reap,

At the wood's boldness by thee blushing stand!

To be so tickled, they would change their state

And situation with those dancing chips,

O'er whom thy fingers walk with gentle gait,

Making dead wood more blest than living lips.

    Since saucy jacks so happy are in this,

    Give them thy fingers, me thy lips to kiss.

128

你是我的乐神，我的音乐演奏师，

每当你的玉指轻柔地弹奏键盘，

那幸运的琴键发出甜美的乐声，

清脆的和弦悦耳动听，沁人心脾，

此刻，我是多么嫉妒那轻盈跳动的琴键

贪婪地亲吻你的柔嫩纤细的芳指！

而我可怜的嘴唇本该获得丰收，

却羞怯地在你身旁瞅着它们肆无忌惮。

我的嘴唇受到如此挑逗，心痒难忍，

渴望同那些欢跳的琴键换位，

你的手指在琴键上轻盈地跃动，

让那些死木片比活嘴唇还幸福。

　　既然那些放肆的木片对此高兴不已，

　　那你就索性把手指给它们，把芳唇给我。

129

The expense of spirit in a waste of shame

Is lust in action; and till action, lust

Is perjured, murderous, bloody, full of blame,

Savage, extreme, rude, cruel, not to trust,

Enjoy'd no sooner but despisèd straight;

Past reason hunted, and no sooner had

Past reason hated, as a swallow'd bait

On purpose laid to make the taker mad;

Mad in pursuit and in possession so;

Had, having, and in quest to have, extreme;

A bliss in proof, and proved, a very woe;

Before, a joy proposed; behind, a dream.

    All this the world well knows; yet none knows well

    To shun the heaven that leads men to this hell.

129

把精力耗尽于一片羞言的荒原，

纵情食色，沉迷于温柔乡野。

为填欲壑不惜说谎、谋杀，恶贯满盈，

野蛮暴戾，心狠手辣，背信弃义。

欢娱未已，便觉索然无味，

疯狂寻觅，又疯狂憎弃，

犹如吞下故意令其疯狂的诱饵，

疯狂追逐，疯狂占有。

过去要，现在要，将来还要，贪婪至极，

刚才尚觉得幸福无限，

转瞬便盈盈一腔愁绪。

云前一晌贪欢，雨后一场梦断。

　　尘世对这一切尽人皆知，

　　怎奈没人知道如何躲避这通往地狱的天堂！

130

My mistress' eyes are nothing like the sun;

Coral is far more red than her lips' red;

If snow be white, why then her breasts are dun;

If hairs be wires, black wires grow on her head.

I have seen roses damask'd, red and white,

But no such roses see I in her cheeks;

And in some perfumes is there more delight

Than in the breath that from my mistress reeks.

I love to hear her speak, yet well I know

That music hath a far more pleasing sound;

I grant I never saw a goddess go,

My mistress, when she walks, treads on the ground.

And yet, by heaven, I think my love as rare

As any she belied with false compare.

130

我情人的眼睛一点也不像太阳；

她的朱唇也远比不上珊瑚红靓；

她的酥胸也不及雪白而暗淡无光；

她满头黑丝，并非金发①长长；

我见过美丽似锦的玫瑰红白两色相得益彰，

此种娇艳美色却无缘我情人的脸庞。

我曾闻到过各种怡人的气味飘香，

可我情人口中却如荼蘼开过味无芬芳。

我倒是喜欢听她说话的声音，

可与悦耳的音乐相比则异如天壤。

我虽没有见过仙女行步时的曼妙，

而我的情人走路时震得地面咚咚作响。

　　老天为证，我的爱人也是世间奇珍，

　　毫不逊色那些号称佳丽的美艳绝伦。

---

① 莎士比亚时代的英国人认为金发比黑发漂亮。——译者注

131

Thou art as tyrannous, so as thou art,

As those whose beauties proudly make them cruel;

For well thou know'st to my dear doting heart

Thou art the fairest and most precious jewel.

Yet, in good faith, some say that thee behold

Thy face hath not the power to make love groan;

To say they err I dare not be so bold,

Although I swear it to myself alone.

And, to be sure that is not false I swear,

A thousand groans, but thinking on thy face,

One on another's neck, do witness bear

Thy black is fairest in my judgment's place.

    In nothing art thou black save in thy deeds,

    And thence this slander, as I think, proceeds.

131

你有什么资本也像她们那样跋扈？

人家骄横是因为自己美色绝伦。

你深知我爱你如痴如醉，

视你为世上最美最贵的奇珍。

可是说心里话，见过你的人说，

你的脸没有让人看了发出惊呼的魅力。

尽管我心里骂他们一派胡言，

可我不敢公开指责他们是信口开河。

我发誓我的话不掺半点假，

一想到你的脸我心就惊叹万千，

不绝于口地为我作证，

你的黑色在我眼中娇美绝伦。

　　　其实你一点也不黑，只是有点专横，

　　　我想，就是因为这一点，诽谤才四处流行。

132

Thine eyes I love, and they, as pitying me,

Knowing thy heart torments me with disdain,

Have put on black and loving mourners be,

Looking with pretty ruth upon my pain.

And truly not the morning sun of heaven

Better becomes the grey cheeks of the east,

Nor that full star that ushers in the even

Doth half that glory to the sober west,

As those two mourning eyes become thy face:

O, let it then as well beseem thy heart

To mourn for me, since mourning doth thee grace,

And suit thy pity like in every part.

      Then will I swear beauty herself is black,

      And all they foul that thy complexion lack.

132

我爱你那双同情我的眼睛，

它们知道你内心对我鄙夷无情，

于是穿上丧服诚如痴情的哀悼者，

以悲悯同情的目光看我痛苦万分。

其实，即使天空冉冉升起的旭日

把东方飘飞的白云染成绯红，

即使伴随夜幕降临而升起的金星

让西方清冷的长空熠熠生辉，

都不如你镶着这双哀伤眼睛的脸美艳！

噢，既然哀伤会让你变得更美，

那就让你的心也来为我哀悼，

让它也穿上丧服为我表达哀伤。

　　于是我会发誓说黑本身就是美，

　　没有黝黑的肤色逞谈美艳。

133

Beshrew that heart that makes my heart to groan

For that deep wound it gives my friend and me!

Is't not enough to torture me alone,

But slave to slavery my sweet'st friend must be?

Me from myself thy cruel eye hath taken,

And my next self thou harder hast engross'd,

Of him, myself, and thee I am forsaken;

A torment thrice threefold thus to be cross'd.

Prison my heart in thy steel bosom's ward,

But then my friend's heart let my poor heart bail;

Whoe'er keeps me, let my heart be his guard;

Thou canst not then use rigor in my gaol.

    And yet thou wilt; for I, being pent in thee,

    Perforce am thine, and all that is in me.

133

你那颗把我心伤透的心真该死，

因为它不只伤害了我还伤害了我的朋友。

难道你折磨我一个人还不够，

还非得要让我的好友也深受你的奴役？

你冷酷的眼睛早已让我魂不附体，

你如此狠心，将另一个我也不放过。

这样他和你以及我自己都抛弃了我，

如此，我要经受三重折磨。

请你把我的心囚禁在你铁石般的心房，

让我这颗不幸的心做抵押将朋友的心保释，

不管谁囚禁我，我心都要把朋友保护，

这样你就不会在狱中对他施暴。

　　而你依然会对我施暴，因为我还囚禁在你心里，

　　不过，我本属于你，我的一切都归你。

134

So, now I have confess'd that he is thine,

And I myself am mortgag'd to thy will,

Myself I'll forfeit, so that other mine

Thou wilt restore, to be my comfort still.

But thou wilt not, nor he will not be free,

For thou art covetous and he is kind;

He learn'd but surety-like to write for me

Under that bond that him as fast doth bind.

The statute of thy beauty thou wilt take,

Thou usurer, that put'st forth all to use,

And sue a friend came debtor for my sake;

So him I lose through my unkind abuse.

    Him have I lost; thou hast both him and me;

    He pays the whole, and yet am I not free.

134

既然我承认他也已经属于你，

且为满足你这欲念将自己抵押，

我心甘情愿地放弃我自己，

以便你能将另一个我释放，让其自由自在。

可是你不放过他，他也不想逃脱你而觅自由，

因为你贪欲无度，而他善解人意；

他本是要为我担保才在契约上签字，

不成想这契约却紧紧地把他束缚。

你根据你的美貌契据任意把抵押物使用，

你这唯利是图的高利贷放贷人，

让我的朋友也因我成了欠你债的人，

我因对他不仁不义而把他失去。

　　　我失去了他，你却把我们俩全都占有，

　　　他还了欠你的债，我却依然未获自由。

135

Whoever hath her wish, thou hast thy Will,

And Will to boot, and Will in overplus;

More than enough am I that vex thee still,

To thy sweet will making addition thus.

Wilt thou, whose will is large and spacious,

Not once vouchsafe to hide my will in thine?

Shall will in others seem right gracious,

And in my will no fair acceptance shine?

The sea all water, yet receives rain still

And in abundance addeth to his store;

So thou, being rich in Will, add to thy Will

One will of mine, to make thy large Will more.

    Let no unkind, no fair beseechers kill;

    Think all but one, and me in that one Will.

135

只要她所想，你就应有所欲，

欲壑难填，欲火难熄。

我总是让你心神不宁，

却能遂你甜美之欲。

而你欲念如此漭弥，

还不许将吾欲隐藏其中，

难道他人之欲就如此怡人，

而我之欲就如此俗不可纳？

瀛水茫茫，依然纳雨不止，

使其更加浩瀚充盈；

所以，尽管你欲丰盈，

但纳吾欲会使你欲丰盈有加。

切勿再无情地让仰慕者灰心意冷，

万欲皆归一欲，吾欲亦欲海一粟。

136

If thy soul cheque thee that I come so near,

Swear to thy blind soul that I was thy Will,

And will, thy soul knows, is admitted there;

Thus far for love my love-suit, sweet, fulfil.

'Will' will fulfil the treasure of thy love,

Ay, fill it full with wills, and my will one.

In things of great receipt with ease we prove

Among a number one is reckon'd none.

Then in the number let me pass untold,

Though in thy stores' account I one must be;

For nothing hold me, so it please thee hold

That nothing me, a something sweet to thee.

    Make but my name thy love, and love that still,

    And then thou lovest me, for my name is 'Will.'

136

如果你的灵魂指责我与你太亲密，

就对你那瞎眼的灵魂说我本是你心欲。

你的灵魂应知道欲在此，理当被准入，

为了爱你应让我饥渴的欲尝到甜蜜。

此欲一定会填满你爱的宝库，

让欲将你这宝库装满，其中也要有吾欲，

吾欲不过茫茫沧海一粟，

须知沧海纳一滴之雨不费吹灰之力。

把吾欲纳入万欲之中悄悄进入你爱的宝库，

且理应列在你的宝物账单里。

我虽微不足道，但对填你欲壑重要无比，

即使吾渺小亦请收纳，那会使你幸福甜蜜。

　　　让我的欲名成你之爱，爱它到永远，

　　　爱它就是爱本人，本人欲名即心欲①。

---

① 莎士比亚的名 Willam 缩写 Will 意即 "欲望"。——译者注

137

Thou blind fool, Love, what dost thou to mine eyes,

That they behold, and see not what they see?

They know what beauty is, see where it lies,

Yet what the best is take the worst to be.

If eyes, corrupt by over-partial looks,

Be anchor'd in the bay where all men ride,

Why of eyes' falsehood hast thou forged hooks,

Whereto the judgment of my heart is tied?

Why should my heart think that a several plot

Which my heart knows the wide world's common place?

Or mine eyes, seeing this, say this is not,

To put fair truth upon so foul a face?

  In things right true my heart and eyes have err'd,

  And to this false plague are they now transferr'd.

137

眼瞎脑笨的爱神，你对我的眼睛施了什么法术？

它们大大地瞪着，却什么也看不见。

它们原本知道什么是美，美在何方，

如今却把美丑颠倒，善恶错位。

如果说眼睛被偏见所蒙蔽。

而误入人人都可停泊的港湾，

你为什么还用我眼睛的错觉锻造神钩，

把我心的判断力紧紧勾住不放？

我心虽然明知那里是人人可至的众人之所，

为何错将其当成少数人的私第？

为何我的眼睛虽见真相，却不道实情，

反用真美去粉饰掩盖如此丑陋的嘴脸？

　　我的心和眼美丑颠倒，真假不辨，

　　以至于染上了这骗人的瘟病。

138

When my love swears that she is made of truth,

I do believe her, though I know she lies,

That she might think me some untutor'd youth,

Unlearned in the world's false subtleties.

Thus vainly thinking that she thinks me young,

Although she knows my days are past the best,

Simply I credit her false-speaking tongue;

On both sides thus is simple truth suppressed.

But wherefore says she not she is unjust?

And wherefore say not I that I am old?

O, love's best habit is in seeming trust,

And age in love loves not to have years told.

     Therefore I lie with her and she with me,

     And in our faults by lies we flatter'd be.

138

每当吾爱发誓说她忠贞无比，
我明知她在撒谎也佯装信以为真，
以让她觉得我还是个无知的少年，
不知这世上布满骗人的诡计。
于是我徒然认为她当真以为我年轻
尽管早已过芳春年华她心知肚明。
我天真地相信她满口的谎言，
所以她和我都把实情隐瞒。
她为何不说她未道实情？
我为何不说我已不年轻？
爱的外衣就是表面信赖，
芳春已过的恋人耻谈年龄。
　　因此我对她撒谎，她对我隐瞒，
　　我们在相互欺骗中各自心欢。

139

O, call not me to justify the wrong

That thy unkindness lays upon my heart;

Wound me not with thine eye but with thy tongue;

Use power with power and slay me not by art.

Tell me thou lovest elsewhere, but in my sight,

Dear heart, forbear to glance thine eye aside:

What need'st thou wound with cunning when thy might

Is more than my o'er-press'd defense can bide?

Let me excuse thee: "ah! my love well knows

Her pretty looks have been mine enemies."

And therefore from my face she turns my foes,

That they elsewhere might dart their injuries.

    Yet do not so; but since I am near slain,

    Kill me outright with looks and rid my pain.

139

噢，别指望我原谅你的恶行，

你无情无义伤透了我的心。

你可暴口伤我，而切莫用眼神，

你伤害我可竭尽你的全力，但切勿耍诡计。

心肝儿，你可以直接说你已移情别至，

但不要在我眼皮底下向别人送秋波。

你力量强大我无力抵挡你的伤害，

那你何必还要暗地里费尽心机？

让我来为你辩解吧："我的心肝儿，

她深信自己迷人的眼神是我的劲敌"

所以才从我的脸上转移到我的情敌，

像飞箭一样又射向和伤害别人。

　　千万不要那样，反正我已是奄奄一息，

　　你干脆用眼神把我杀死，让我把痛苦消靡。

140

Be wise as thou art cruel; do not press

My tongue-tied patience with too much disdain;

Lest sorrow lend me words and words express

The manner of my pity-wanting pain.

If I might teach thee wit, better it were,

Though not to love, yet, love, to tell me so;

As testy sick men, when their deaths be near,

No news but health from their physicians know;

For if I should despair, I should grow mad,

And in my madness might speak ill of thee:

Now this ill-wresting world is grown so bad,

Mad slanderers by mad ears believèd be,

   That I may not be so, nor thou belied,

   Bear thine eyes straight, though thy proud heart go wide.

140

你即使不仁不义那也应当放聪明些,

不要步步紧逼,让我缄口忍耐你太多的侮辱,

以免深愁生怨言,怨言催呐喊,

诉说我渴望怜悯的痛苦;

如果你跟我学聪明些,即使你不爱我

你也最好言不由衷地说爱我深深,

就像乖戾的病人,虽然濒临死期,

却只想听医生说他很快就会痊愈。

否则,如果令我绝望,我会变得疯狂,

疯狂中可能会将你的劣迹公之于众。

如今这世界欺世盗名已然成风,

疯狂的耳朵愿相信疯狂的谣言。

　　但愿我不疯狂,你不被诽谤,

　　你要直视我的眼睛,即使你春心放浪。

141

In faith, I do not love thee with mine eyes,

For they in thee a thousand errors note;

But 'tis my heart that loves what they despise,

Who in despite of view is pleased to dote.

Nor are mine ears with thy tongue's tune delighted,

Nor tender feeling, to base touches prone,

Nor taste, nor smell, desire to be invited

To any sensual feast with thee alone.

But my five wits nor my five senses can

Dissuade one foolish heart from serving thee,

Who leaves unsway'd the likeness of a man,

Thy proud hearts slave and vassal wretch to be.

> Only my plague thus far I count my gain,

> That she that makes me sin, awards me pain.

141

说实话，我的眼睛并不喜欢你，

因为它们看你全身是斑斑劣迹。

虽然眼睛嫌弃，心却爱你无比，

不顾眼睛所见，对你痴情不已。

我的耳朵也不欣赏你的歌喉，

我敏感的触觉也不愿抚摸你的身体，

味觉和嗅觉也避你三舍，

不愿光临你举办的感官盛席。

不论我的五智①还是我的五官，

都不能阻止我的痴心去侍奉你，

只留下一个人形的躯体，

我的心成了你春心的侍从与奴隶。

　　　我的痴情病也让我获益良多：

　　　她之于我，诱之以罪，授之以苦。

---

① 五智：西方的五智指常识、鉴赏力、想象力、判断力和记忆力。——译者注

142

Love is my sin, and thy dear virtue hate,

Hate of my sin, grounded on sinful loving.

O, but with mine compare thou thine own state,

And thou shalt find it merits not reproving;

Or, if it do, not from those lips of thine,

That have profan'd their scarlet ornaments

And seal'd false bonds of love as oft as mine,

Robb'd others' beds' revenues of their rents.

Be it lawful I love thee, as thou lovest those

Whom thine eyes woo as mine importune thee.

Root pity in thy heart, that when it grows

Thy pity may deserve to pitied be.

    If thou dost seek to have what thou dost hide,

    By self-example mayst thou be denied!

142

爱你是我之罪，恨我爱你是你之德，
你恨我之罪源于我对你的有罪之爱。
噢，你若处在我的位置想想，
会发现你恨我毫无理由，
就算有，也不应出自你的口。
那样就亵渎了你的唇红，如同在伪爱誓约上
盖的印记——当然我也经常如此——
在他人府邸的床笫偷欢。
犹如你爱别人，我爱你也一样合法，
我两眼焦渴地凝望着你，你却深情地凝望别人，
让怜爱在你心中生根吧，一旦发芽开花，
你的怜爱就会收到同样的回报——怜爱。
　　　你把自己的爱怜深藏，却只向别人索取，
　　　别人也会效仿你，以牙还牙将你拒。

143

Lo, as a careful housewife runs to catch
One of her feather'd creatures broke away,
Sets down her babe, and makes all swift dispatch
In pursuit of the thing she would have stay;
Whilst her neglected child holds her in chase,
Cries to catch her whose busy care is bent
To follow that which flies before her face,
Not prizing her poor infant's discontent;
So run'st thou after which flies from thee,
Whilst I thy babe chase these afar behind;
But if thou catch thy hope, turn back to me,
And play the mother's part, kiss me, be kind.
    So will I pray thou mayst have thy Will,
    If thou turn back and my loud crying still.

143

瞧！多像一个细心的家庭主妇

在追赶从鸡舍逃走的一只公鸡。

放下抱在怀里的孩子匆匆而去，

穷追不舍要抓到她早已企冀的东西。

被她丢下那没人管的孩子紧随其后，

哭喊着追她，她却只顾向前箭步如飞，

紧追那只从她眼皮底下溜掉的公鸡，

毫不理会她那可怜的孩子哭喊焦急。

你也在追赶那个离你而去的东西，

而我就像那个追赶母亲的孩子，

你若如愿以偿，快回头来照看我，

尽母亲职责，吻我，对我温柔体贴。

　　如果你回头照顾我，我会马上停止哭泣，

　　虔诚地为你祈祷，让你满足你的企冀。

144

Two loves I have comfort and despair,

Which like two spirits do suggest me still;

The better angel is a man right fair,

The worser spirit a woman colour'd ill.

To win me soon to hell, my female evil

Tempteth my better angel from my side,

And would corrupt my saint to be devil,

Wooing his purity with her foul pride.

And whether that my angel be turn'd fiend,

Suspect I may, yet not directly tell;

But being both from me, both to each friend,

I guess one angel in another's hell.

Yet this shall I ne'er know, but live in doubt,

Till my bad angel fire my good one out.

144

我有两个爱人——绝望和欢娱，

他们就像两个精灵不断给我下旨意。

善的那一个是个男子，美如天使，

恶的那一个是个女人，丑如魔鬼。

魔鬼为让我尽快坠入地狱，

从我身边将善良的天使引离，

还要把我的天使变成魔鬼，

用其邪恶的风骚玷污天使的纯真。

我的天使会否变成了魔鬼，

我只能猜测，但难下定论。

但是他们俩成了朋友，都从我身边离去。

所以我猜，善良的天使也坠入了地狱。

　　不过实情我难以知晓，永远成迷，

　　除非魔鬼用火将天使逐出了地狱。

145

Those lips that Love's own hand did make,

Breathèd forth the sound that said "I hate",

To me that languish'd for her sake;

But when she saw my woeful state,

Straight in her heart did mercy come,

Chiding that tongue that ever sweet

Was us'd in giving gentle doom.

And taught it thus anew to greet.

'I hate' she alter'd with an end,

That followed it as gentle day

Doth follow night, who, like a fiend

From heaven to hell is flown away.

    "I hate", from hate away she threw,

    And sav'd my life, saying "not you".

145

我的爱神亲手为吾爱造了两片朱唇①，

我深陷情迷，为伊消得人憔悴②，

双唇冲着我猛然说"我恨！"

可当她看到我悲愁不已，

怜悯之心油然而起，

责怪她那一贯甜蜜的口唇，

要它们说话用委婉的口吻，

并要学会礼貌待人。

于是她改口说"我恨"，

说完后面又补充了半句，

顿时像黑夜后迎来曙光万里，

让魔鬼般的黑夜从天堂逃遁至地狱。

　　　她在"我恨"之后补充说"不是你"，

　　　犹如救我于水深火热，给我浓浓爱意。

---

① 该诗原文为四音步抑扬格，不同于十四行诗的五音步抑扬格，故此有人认为此诗非莎士
比亚的作品。——译者注

② 借用柳永词句译意。——译者注

146

Poor soul, the centre of my sinful earth,

Fool'd by these rebel powers that thee array,

Why dost thou pine within and suffer dearth,

Painting thy outward walls so costly gay?

Why so large cost, having so short a lease,

Dost thou upon thy fading mansion spend?

Shall worms, inheritors of this excess,

Eat up thy charge? Is this thy body's end?

Then soul, live thou upon thy servant's loss,

And let that pine to aggravate thy store;

Buy terms divine in selling hours of dross;

Within be fed, without be rich no more.

> So shalt thou feed on Death, that feed on men,

> And Death once dead, there's no more dying then.

146

可怜的灵魂——我罪恶肉体的中心，

你把叛逆之躯乔装打扮而受其愚弄。

你为何在躯体内忍受着饥寒与悲苦，

还把这外壳粉饰得如此华美？

这摇摇欲坠的屋宇①，租期短暂，

租金高昂，你为何还不惜重金为其装潢？

最终还不是尸虫把你豪奢殿堂继承，

任由它们饕餮挥霍？那就是你贵体的归宿！

灵魂呀，那时你只好靠肉体的损耗来度日，

以身体消瘦来增加和丰富你的储藏；

抛售那些短暂无益的快乐时光，购买生命的永恒吧，

让灵魂获得滋养，别再管外表如何堂皇。

　　如此，你将会吃掉吃人的死神，

　　死神一死，人间再无死亡降临。

---

① 喻指人的躯体。在第十三首也曾用过这样的比喻。——译者注

147

My love is as a fever, longing still,

For that which longer nurseth the disease;

Feeding on that which doth preserve the ill,

The uncertain sickly appetite to please.

My reason, the physician to my love,

Angry that his prescriptions are not kept,

Hath left me, and I desperate now approve

Desire is death, which physic did except.

Past cure I am, now Reason is past care,

And frantic-mad with evermore unrest;

My thoughts and my discourse as madmen's are,

At random from the truth vainly express'd;

　　For I have sworn thee fair, and thought thee bright,

　　Who art black as hell, as dark as night.

147

我的爱就像患了一场热病，

总是渴望被人呵护无止境，

于是便服用丹药来维持病症，

以便让满足病态般的过分需要得逞。

理智是我这热病的主治医生，

他对我未遵医嘱非常气愤，

于是便愤然离去，我在绝望中明白：

欲望即死亡，乃医病之大忌。

现在理智已离我而去，我已无药可救，

陷入烦躁狂妄，终日不得安宁，

思维和语言同疯人一样不切实际，

思维充斥妄想，言语充斥癫狂。

　　　因为我曾说你娇美，也认为你靓丽，

　　　可你却黑若夜幕，暗若地狱。

148

O me! What eyes hath Love put in my head,

Which have no correspondence with true sight;

Or, if they have, where is my judgment fled,

That censures falsely what they see aright?

If that be fair whereon my false eyes dote,

What means the world to say it is not so?

If it be not, then love doth well denote

Love's eye is not so true as men's: no,

How can it? O! how can Love's eye be true,

That is so vexed with watching and with tears?

No marvel then, though I mistake my view;

The sun itself sees not, till heaven clears.

    O cunning Love! With tears thou keep'st me blind,

    Lest eye well-seeing thy foul faults should find.

148

天哪！爱神在我头上安了双什么眼睛，

它们所见怎么与实情大相径庭？

如果说它们所见是真，那我的判断力情何以堪，

它怎么会把眼睛所见实情判定为虚假？

如果我虚妄的眼睛所迷恋的是美丽，

那世人为什么偏要说它丑陋无比？

如果眼睛所见不美，那么爱就是在明确暗示

情人的眼睛不及世人眼睛明亮，为何如此？

因为受渴望目光和如泉泪水双重困扰，

爱的眼睛怎么能够看得真实可信？

所以即使我看不准也没有什么稀奇，

就算太阳也只在晴日才能明察万物。

　　狡黠的爱呀，你用眼泪模糊我的眼睛，

　　唯恐我能把你丑陋的缺陷看清。

149

Canst thou, O cruel! Say I love thee not,

When I against myself with thee partake?

Do I not think on thee, when I forgot

Am of my self, all tyrant, for thy sake?

Who hateth thee that I do call my friend?

On whom frown'st thou that I do fawn upon,

Nay , if thou lour'st on me, do I not spend

Revenge upon myself with present moan?

What merit do I in my self respect,

That is so proud thy service to despise,

When all my best doth worship thy defect,

Command by the motion of thine eyes?

     But, love, hate on, for now I know thy mind;

     Those that can see thou lov'st, and I am blind.

149

狠心的人儿，你怎么能说我不爱你？

为了你，我都与你一道与自己过不去。

我的独裁者，为了你我都害了相思病，

甚至我都全然忘记了自己是何人。

我恨你之所恨，从未以之为友，

我憎你之所憎，从未对其献媚。

不仅如此，只要你对我皱眉表示不满，

我就立刻对自己深深地自责和悔恨。

屈身侍奉你我倍感骄傲，

对你的缺点我不遗余力地崇拜，

你使一个眼神儿我便惟命是从，

难道这些优点还不值得你肯定？

　　　　爱呀，恨我吧，我现在看透了你的心，

　　　　你爱那些看着你漂亮的人，而我是盲目迷恋你的人。

150

O, from what power hast thou this power might,

With insufficiency my heart to sway?

To make me give the lie to my true sight,

And swear that brightness doth not grace the day?

Whence hast thou this becoming of things ill,

That in the very refuse of thy deeds

There is such strength and warranties of skill,

That, in my mind, thy worst all best exceeds?

Who taught thee how to make me love thee more,

The more I hear and see just cause of hate?

O, though I love what others do abhor,

With others thou shouldst not abhor my state.

    If thy unworthiness rais'd love in me,

    More worthy I to be belov'd of thee.

150

噢！你这无穷魅力从何而来？

即使有缺点也能把我的心主宰。

让我对着亲眼所见脱口撒谎，

让我硬说明媚不会使白天更美。

你从何处得到点石成金的本领？

你那最见不得人的丑行

都显示出你的魅力无穷和手腕神通，

以至于让你的恶行在我心中成了美德。

尽管我亲耳听到或亲眼见到对你恨之有据，

是谁授你秘诀让我对你迷恋不已？

噢，尽管我所爱系他人之所憎，

你也不该与别人一道鄙视我的相思病。

　　　　既然你的缺点都激起我对你的爱，

　　　　那么我对你的爱就更值得你称赞。

151

Love is too young to know what conscience is;

Yet who know not conscience is born of love?

Then, gentle cheater, urge not my amiss,

Lest guilty of my faults thy sweet self prove:

For, thou betraying me, I do betray

My noble part to my gross body's treason;

My soul doth tell my body that he may

Triumph in love; flesh says no farther reason,

But, rising at thy name, doth point out thee

As his triumphant prize. Proud of this pride,

He is contended thy poor drudge to be,

To stand in thy affairs, fall by thy side.

    No want of conscience hold it that I call

    Her "love", for whose dear I rise and fall.

151

年幼的爱神不懂得什么是良心，

可谁不知道良心源于爱心？

所以温柔的骗子可别逼我犯错，

以免让我的罪过成为你风流韵事的证据。

因为你出卖了我，我便把高贵的灵魂

出卖给了水性杨花的肉体。

我的灵魂告诉我的肉体：你可赢得爱情，

可肉体则等不及进一步解释，

一听到你的芳名就起身指向你，

威风凛凛，说你是它在情场赢得的奖赏。

但它甘愿做你的奴隶，无怨无悔，

为爱贴身矗立于你身边，倒下也不分离。

　　我将她称之为爱，并为之肝脑涂地，

　　我坚信，这丝毫不违背良心。

152

In loving thee thou know'st I am forsworn,

But thou art twice forsworn, to me love swearing;

In act thy bed-vow broke, and new faith torn,

In vowing new hate after new love bearing.

But why of two oath's breach do I accuse thee,

When I break twenty? I am perjur'd most;

For all my vows are oaths but to misuse thee,

And all my honest fairs in thee is lost;

For I have sworn deep oaths of thy deep kindness,

Oaths of thy love, thy truth, thy constancy.

And, to enlighten thee, gave eyes to blindness,

Or made them swear against the thing they see;

> For I have sworn thee fair. More perjur'd eye,
>
> To swear against the truth so foul a lie!

152

你知道为了爱你我不惜违背海誓山盟，

可你发誓爱我，却两度毁约。

你已违背婚誓姻盟，又把新约撕毁，

觅得新爱后，便生新恨情。

我已毁约二十次，为何指责你两次毁约？

因为我发誓说的都是违心话，

只是为了把你哄。

因为爱你，我索性抛弃了所有诚信与正直：

我曾信誓旦旦地说你温情善良，

说你情深意切，心诚情真，忠贞不渝，

为说你光彩照人，我说话时闭上眼睛，

或者让眼睛说的违背实情。

　　我曾说对天发誓说你娇美，我的眼睛

　　便瞪着说瞎话，声称我说的都是实情。

153

Cupid laid by his brand and fell asleep.

A maid of Dian's this advantage found,

And his love-kindling fire did quickly steep

In a cold valley-fountain of that ground;

Which borrow'd from this holy fire of Love

A dateless lively heat, still to endure,

And grew a seething bath, which yet men prove

Against strange maladies a sovereign cure.

But at my mistress' eye Love's brand new-fir'd,

The boy for trial needs would touch my breast;

I, sick withal, the help of bath desir'd,

And thither hied, a sad distemper'd guest,

　　But found no cure. The bath for my help lies

　　Where Cupid got new fire — my mistress' eyes.

153

爱神放下手中的火炬进入甜美的梦乡，

月神的一个侍女发现这一天赐良机，

飞快地把爱火熊熊燃烧的火炬拾起，

将其浸入山下幽谷中冰冷的泉水。

清泉从爱神的神圣火焰

获得永不冷却的炽热，弥久绵延，

变成了沸腾激荡的温泉。

有人发现它是能治愈各种怪病的灵丹妙方。

我情人的眼睛把爱神的火炬重新点燃，

为了验证其火力，爱神用它碰碰我的胸膛，

结果我被染病，欲前去温泉寻求医治，

犹如一名悲伤患病的孤客匆匆赶到那里，

  却发现温泉毫无疗效；其实只有我情人的眼睛

  才是治我病患的温泉，因为它们可把爱神的火炬

  重新点燃。

154

The little Love-god lying once asleep

Laid by side his heart-inflaming brand,

Whilst many nymphs that vow'd chaste life to keep

Came tripping by; but in her maiden hand

The fairest votary took up that fire

Which many legions of true hearts had warm'd;

And so the General of hot desire

Was, sleeping, by a virgin hand disarm'd

This brand she quenched in a cool well by,

Which from Love's fire took heat perpetual,

Growing a bath and healthful remedy,

For men diseas'd; but I, my mistress thrall,

　　Came there for cure, and this by that I prove,

　　Love's fire heats water, water cool not love.

154

曾有一次，小爱神进入甜蜜的梦乡，

将那爱情火焰熊熊燃烧的火炬放在了身旁。

一群誓言终身守贞的仙女从这里翩翩走过。

最美的那位用她圣洁的手

将爱神的火炬悄悄拾起，

这火炬可曾温暖过无数人的心田！

这位主宰爱火的司令官，

就这样在睡梦中被少女之手解除了武装。

少女把火炬浸入附近的冷泉将其熄灭，

爱情的炽热便永远留在了圣洁的清泉。

泉水变成了能为人治病的温泉，

因情人令我迷恋不能自拔便去寻求救治；

　　可到了那里却发现了这样一个事实：

　　爱火能使泉水热，泉水难将爱火熄。